ALSO BY HELEN SIMPSON

A Bunch of Fives: Selected Stories

In-Flight Entertainment

In the Driver's Seat

Constitutional

Getting a Life

Dear George

Four Bare Legs in a Bed

COCKFOSTERS

COCKFOSTERS

Stories

Helen Simpson

Alfred A. Knopf

New York · 2017

THIS IS A BORZOI BOOK
PUBLISHED BY ALFRED A. KNOPF

Copyright © 2015 by Helen Simpson

All rights reserved. Published in the United States by
Alfred A. Knopf, a division of Penguin Random House LLC,
New York. Originally published in Great Britain by
Jonathan Cape, an imprint of Vintage Publishing,
a division of Penguin Random House Limited,
London, in 2015.

www.aaknopf.com

Library of Congress Cataloging-in-Publication Data
Names: Simpson, Helen, [date] author.
Title: Cockfosters : stories / Helen Simpson.
Description: New York : Knopf, [2017]
Identifiers: LCCN 2016032867 |
ISBN 9780451493071 (hardcover) |
ISBN 9780451493088 (ebook)
Subjects: | BISAC: FICTION / Literary. |
FICTION / Contemporary Women. |
FICTION / Short Stories (single author).
Classification: LCC PR6069.I4226 A6 2017 |
DDC 823/.914—dc23
LC record available at https://lccn.loc.gov/2016032867

Jacket design by Carol Devine Carson

Manufactured in the United States of America

First United States Edition

Contents

COCKFOSTERS 3

TORREMOLINOS 16

EREWHON 21

KENTISH TOWN 32

KYTHERA 51

MOSCOW 60

CHEAPSIDE 74

ARIZONA 98

BERLIN 118

Acknowledgements 181

COCKFOSTERS

COCKFOSTERS

GREEN PARK

It still might be a disaster but they had silently agreed to take it lightly. As soon as they got off at Green Park Julie realised she'd left them behind on the seat. For a couple of minutes they dithered on the platform wondering what to do, then Philippa had decided: Follow that train! They would hunt them down to the end of the line, always assuming that nobody else was tempted en route to make off with them.

"I mean, why would they," said Julie as they stood crushed shoulder to shoulder on the next train. "They'd be useless to anybody else. And I'm completely lost without them. I can't get used to it!"

"There's no way you're going back to Shropshire without them," said Philippa. "Not with your big Ofsted week coming up."

"It's because they're new," moaned Julie. "I hate them."

"You'll get used to them."

"Not in a million years. Oh, I suppose so. I'm sorry

about the Delacroix," said Julie, as they hunched their shoulders and braced themselves against a fresh crowd surging on at Leicester Square.

"This is better in a way," said Philippa, flashing her a smile. "This way we'll be able to carry on talking."

The two of them had conspired to spend a couple of hours on art, but now that time was promised to the Piccadilly Line. Although they had not seen each other for years, they had instantly been returned to an unstrained intimacy, as unexpected as it was welcome. At school together in south London, they had found it easy to stay in touch in their twenties, and still possible in a shell-shocked way round babies in their early thirties; then Julie and her husband had moved north and it was the roaring forties that had forced friendship to take a back seat in the interests of survival. Now, though, they had started to crawl up out of their burrows, as Philippa put it, and emerge blinking into the sunlight.

COVENT GARDEN

"The worst thing about needing glasses is the bumbling," said Julie. "I've turned into a bumbler overnight. Me! I run marathons!"

They clung on, dodging and twisting as a flood of tourists disgorged itself at Covent Garden.

"I realised what things had come to when I found myself trying to read a map in the rain last time I was on holiday," she continued. "There I was fumbling with my glasses, dropping them, trying and failing to unfold a map I couldn't read, all the time holding an umbrella over my head like a circus clown."

"Look, quick, there's two seats," said Philippa.

"Suddenly I can't see the food on the plate in front of me," ranted Julie. "Not unless I screw one eye up and peer really hard out of the other. I never thought I'd end up gurning at my dinner like a mad pirate. That curry was delicious, by the way."

They had exchanged a decade's worth of high-density news about children and work the night before, Julie as voluble and volatile as ever while Philippa dished up the *rogan josh.*

"Supermarket Special," said Philippa. "I'm too tired to cook by the end of the week. Or the start of it, if I'm honest."

"It was great," said Julie. "The thing is, I don't like wearing them, I don't like the feeling of having a contraption on my face. Imagine kissing someone when you're both wearing glasses—it'd be like the clashing of antlers."

KING'S CROSS ST. PANCRAS

As well as putting the two of them back in touch with each other, Philippa told Julie, her recent forays into Face-book and Friends Reunited had revealed that at least fifty percent of their contemporaries were now unabashedly grey-headed and bespectacled. She herself had had her hair razored into short grey splinters, a look she sought to soften by wearing interesting earrings. Meanwhile Julie's hair, foxy with henna, still touched her shoulders.

"And I've put on a stone in the last year," said Philippa. "I know I should take more exercise. What is it we're supposed to do now? Salsa. Zumba! Line dancing?"

"No, line dancing is a step too far," said Julie. "That's for ten years' time. Yee-ha!"

"Actually, I thought I might try rock climbing," said Philippa shyly.

"Rock climbing?"

"There's a climbing wall just up the road from me in Crystal Palace."

"Use it or lose it!" said Julie, hoping she hadn't let her incredulity show. "That's another reason I don't like glasses—they're no good for anything active like that."

"What about contact lenses?"

"Yeah, I started off with them, but it was like poking myself in the eye every morning getting them in, and just as bad getting them out. Then when I got the knack I found they weren't as good for reading as I'd hoped, and someone at school told me how they cut the oxygen to the cornea and one of his had travelled right up underneath the eyelid towards the back of the eyeball. He'd had to go to hospital to get it taken out so that put me right off. Because whatever you do you mustn't fall asleep when you're wearing them or you'll asphyxiate your eyes."

"Oh, I'm always falling asleep," said Philippa. "I fall asleep at the drop of a hat."

The train had now stopped at King's Cross St. Pancras, and they watched as a young woman struggled to make her way into the crowded compartment with a suitcase and a baby in a sling and two small children.

"I'm very glad I'm not doing that anymore," said Philippa with quiet fervour.

"Yes," said Julie. "I do wonder what happens next, though. Because the current story is, we get more assertive, we cast them all off without a backward glance and move on. We're supposed to leave the nurturing role behind with our oestrogen, see."

"That doesn't sound very likely," said Philippa, considering. "No, I can't see how that would work. They all still really need me. And then, what about the aged parents?"

"Oh, don't," groaned Julie. "I'm up and down the M1 like a yo-yo."

HOLLOWAY ROAD

Philippa was telling Julie more about her internet discoveries. She had tracked down a surprising number of their old classmates from the school they had attended together in New Addington. Suzanne Fowler had married the boy with the car who used to pick her up at the school gates, she'd gone into nursing then had three children and now she was divorced. Hilary Trundle, who'd left after O levels to work in Dolcis, was on tamoxifen for breast cancer, she'd set up a blog about it. And Tina Jakes, having TEFLed her way round most of southeast Asia, was running a martial arts centre in Thornton Heath.

"Tina Jakes? The netball queen?"

"That's the one."

"THIS is a Piccadilly Line train to Cockfosters," declared a loud voice, and they stopped talking while it repeated its assertion.

"Piccadilly," said Julie dreamily. "Piccadilly. Accommodation! Do you remember the time they got that woman from the secretarial college to come and give us a talk? That was the third option, wasn't it, if you couldn't face teaching or nursing. Do you remember, she held out the carrot that one day you might work your way up to be personal assistant to a very important man! Talk about the glittering prizes."

"We were being trained to serve others," commented Philippa. "That was what it was."

"She also warned us there were certain words which were hard to spell, that no decent secretary would bring shame on herself by getting 'Piccadilly' or 'accommodation' wrong."

"Double *c* double *m*?" said Philippa. "Only three of us went on to university. That was normal then, of course."

"And as soon as we left uni computers came in and that was the end of that," continued Julie. "Secretaries are like coal miners now, aren't they; they're a dying breed. We're not fifty yet but when you think of it, not having had email in our youth makes us positively antediluvian."

"Oh, good word! You can tell you did English."

"Yeah, I can spell it," growled Julie. "I just can't read it."

"Of course you could always get them lasered," said Philippa. "Though my deputy head had it done and she said you have to stay awake during it with your eyelids pulled apart by clamps and there's a terrible smell of burning."

"Ugh! Like that film with the eyeball and the razor-blade. What was it called? You know. Black and white, French; a cloud goes over the moon."

"I don't know."

"It'll come to me," said Julie grimly.

ARSENAL

"I can't bear to think how much they cost," said Julie. "And then to lose them . . . Remember that poem about losing stuff? Her mother's watch, de da de da. But I've forgotten who it's by. I really am losing it."

"You haven't lost them," said Philippa. "They'll be waiting for us at Cockfosters."

"The optician told me that forty-seven is when it happens; that's the average age for when your eyes go and it was spot-on for me," said Julie. "The money I've handed over to that man in the last year!"

They fell silent as the train picked up speed on its reckless way out of Arsenal, rattling all over as it belted them along.

I've always been a bit of a loser, thought Julie; the year

I was eleven I left my swimming bag on the bus almost every Thursday. She cast back to the sensation of her chlorinated hair in a dripping elastic-banded ponytail on the long crawl back to recover the bag from the bus depot. Then there were all the keys over the years, not to mention the gloves . . . I've been doing this ever since I can remember, she thought; it's good practice for the future I suppose, though I still haven't got used to it after all this time.

TURNPIKE LANE

The crowds had thinned out and their carriage was only half full.

"You know those feelings we're supposed to start feeling now?" said Julie, off on another track. "You know, now they're off at uni, what are we here for if we're not able to have babies anymore—now that we've probably only got one or two chances to have a last one?"

"Perish the thought."

"Well I'm not," continued Julie.

"You mean, mourning the loss of fertility?" said Philippa cautiously.

"Yes. That. I've figured it's OK as long as it doesn't go hand in glove with the loss of, um, sex."

"Oh I don't know," said Philippa.

"No?"

"He's so grumpy. You saw what he was like last night

when you arrived, he wouldn't look away from the football to say hello until I gave him a shove."

"He was just tired."

"No, he's always like that."

"Elizabeth Bishop!" said Julie. "That's who wrote that poem. I knew it would come to me."

"Well done," said Philippa.

BOUNDS GREEN

A little after Bounds Green the train surged into daylight for the first time, and they could see house roofs and a little gasworks through the window.

"When Ellie went to Leeds Met, we decided to split up for a while," said Philippa. "We didn't move out or anything, that would have been too expensive, but we gave each other space, if you get my meaning."

"Oh, I'm sorry."

"No it's all right, we decided to stay together in the end, we're going to Thailand at Christmas. But it was an *interesting* time. First thing he did was join a website called NewPartner.com. It wasn't hard to guess his password so I used to log on to his computer every day, have a look at the women who'd winked him . . ."

"*Winked* him?"

". . . technical term. Then I'd turn his score back to zero."

"Wow," said Julie.

"I know him," shrugged Philippa. "He'd described himself as athletic and toned, like all the other men coming up to fifty; whereas the women—also self-deluded, equally so—said they liked walks in the rain and going to the cinema."

"Really?"

"But they *don't* like going to the cinema, do you get what I'm saying; the most they can manage is a DVD on a Saturday night with a takeaway."

ARNOS GROVE

"I can't really see what's out there anymore," said Julie, peering through the window. "That's as well as not being able to read or tell whether it's a bee or a wasp."

"You need varifocals," said Philippa.

"That's what I've got," said Julie. "Or rather, what I had."

"My mother says they changed her life, but you can't walk downstairs in them, and if you go to the theatre you have to sit in the stalls not the circle."

"Why?"

"I don't know. But it's very expensive."

"What I want is what I had before. I want to be able to read a book *and* see out of the window. I know, I know; if I get them back I really ought to wear them all the time. It just seems a shame to spoil what little I've got left. Vanity!"

"Why don't you decide to enjoy it?" suggested Philippa. "Nobody notices a middle-aged woman in glasses, you could get away with murder."

"True," laughed Julie.

OAKWOOD

The train had slowed to a rest outside Oakwood station. They sat gazing at a group of silver birches on a cutting between the railway tracks.

"It's annoying not knowing how long we've got left, don't you think?" said Julie.

"Thirty years," said Philippa. "Forty!"

"Or ten," said Julie. "Or two. It would be good to know on some level, sort of subconsciously, don't you think? In order to pace ourselves. It would be so useful when it came to money, for example, knowing whether you ought to be worrying about your pension or if you knew you'd only got a year left you could blow it all on a really good holiday."

"A bit depressing, though, the holiday, if you knew what was coming next?"

"Well, it would have to be subconscious, the knowledge," said Julie. "Obviously."

A voice boomed out over the speaker system: "The next station is Cockfosters. This train will terminate there. Please ensure you take all your personal belongings with you."

"*Now* they tell me. But Philippa, the more I think about it, the more I see it's up to us to get on and plan lovely times and do what we want to do because any minute now we could be disabled with a stroke, paralysed from the neck down!"

"A stroke?" chortled Philippa. "Why not a heart attack or cancer?"

"It was in the paper yesterday," admitted Julie. "You can't always tell if someone's had a stroke so you have to ask them to stick their tongue out. That's the latest test for it."

COCKFOSTERS

As the train drew in to its destination, they were giggling and sticking their tongues out at each other like the silly schoolgirls they had once been together.

Waiting on the platform were more than half a dozen cleaners with plastic bags and pincers poised to clear the carriages.

"They look efficient," said Philippa, impressed.

"Very."

"It obviously happens all the time, people forgetting stuff, leaving stuff behind."

"*Un Chien Andalou!*" cried Julie. "*That* was the film I was telling you about!"

And she punched the air in triumph.

"Well done," said Philippa.

By the time they had managed to recover the lost varifocals from the supervisor's office, their spirits were high and still rising. Sunlight flooded the station concourse and stopped them in their tracks for a moment. They stood side by side, blinking, smiling.

"This train will terminate here," came a station announcement. "Cockfosters station. This is the end of the line."

"But not for us," quipped Philippa, laughing, patting her friend's arm.

Then, once they had paused to check the departures board, they hurried over to the far platform where the next train stood in readiness, ticking over, waiting to take them back into town.

TORREMOLINOS

There was some sort of commotion in the corridor, then a bed was wheeled into the space beside me. The man on the bed eyed me sideways from his pillow and I eyed him from mine.

"You look a bit rough, mate," he said after a while.

I thought, I could say the same about *you*, mate; that's a nasty bruise you've got on your face. Instead, I croaked, "Not as rough as I was." Which was true.

"What you in for then?" said the man.

"Triple bypass," I said. "They call it cabbage."

"Cabbage?" he said.

"That's what the doctors call it," I said. "Cabbage surgery."

I felt tired and closed my eyes. I must have drifted off. When I came to I saw that the man was still watching me from his pillow.

"All right then?" he said.

"Yes thanks," I managed.

"Thing is," he said, lowering his voice so I could only just hear, "Thing is, I come in from next door."

"Next door?"

"The Scrubs," he said, in the same low voice.

This hospital's beside the prison, I thought; of course it is. I was still coming down from my near-death experience. I had tubes coming out all over the place.

"What are *you* in for then?" I asked, seeing as he'd asked me.

"GBH," he said.

"No, I didn't mean *that*," I said, a bit confused.

"Eight years," he said.

"You were stitched up?" I suggested.

"You could say that," he said. "Yeah."

"So was I!" I said. "That makes two of us. No, I mustn't laugh, ow, I'll come apart."

At this point he started chuckling: hur-hur-hur.

As I lay there trying to hold my insides in and not laugh, there came into my mind the terror I'd felt as a child when my father was reading to me one time, about a boy in a graveyard and a villain saying, "I'll have your heart and liver out." Something like that.

"Tell the truth," said the man, "I told 'em I was having a heart attack."

"Oh," I said.

"Yeah," he said. "Look mate, do me a favour."

"What?"

"Tell me what it's like."

"What, a heart attack?" I said.

"Yeah. So I can tell the doctors when they get round to me. Then they'll have to keep me in for tests."

"Oh," I said, and stopped to think about this.

"I needed a break," he said.

Fair enough, I thought; fair enough.

"At first it's like a finger," I said. "Pressing very hard in your chest so you can't breathe. There's a pain in your left shoulder, then it spreads, the pain, up your neck to your jaw."

"Your jaw," he said, stroking his stubble thoughtfully.

"Yes. It's like a vice. You're being squeezed in a vice and it's making you break out in a muck sweat."

I didn't like to remember it.

"That's good," he said. "Like a vice. Thanks."

He rolled his head on the pillow and stared up at the ceiling.

"What's it like then?" I said after a while. "Next door?"

He turned his big expressionless face my way again.

"Boring," he said at last.

"Tell them your old man died of a heart attack," I said. "Because it's often something that's in the family."

"He did an' all."

"Play that up. And, sorry if this sounds a bit personal, but you're quite big too."

"Twenty stone."

"That's good. So if they ask, tell them you like fry-ups and salt with everything."

"Then I won't be telling no lies, will I," he said.

"Right," I said, closing my eyes.

I realised I was exhausted. I still couldn't get used to

this being me, this poor old creature on the bed, rib cage held together with wire, left leg heavily bandaged.

The night before the operation, once I'd signed a form saying it was nobody's fault if I died, and once the surgeon had told me my heart was the same size as a clenched fist—yes, how strange. So. Once they'd all gone, I was lying in bed looking at a beautiful tree I could see through the window where it was waving its branches slowly in the wind, and I thought about my life, all the nice things I'd done.

Then afterwards, when I woke up, I had a big tube in my throat, which was something I'd been frightened of happening. I'd had a real dread of waking up to find myself on a ventilator with a tube down my throat. The nurse brought me a pen and paper and I wrote *How long tube in?* She told me, ten minutes. But very soon after that she took the tube out and I knew I could stop worrying.

Next, though I don't remember this, I wrote *I'm so happy* and tore the sheet of paper off the pad and gave it to her; and I kept on doing this, she told me, sheet after sheet, till it was finished.

I opened my eyes now and saw my neighbour was still watching me.

"Looks like you had a nice little kip," he said, almost tenderly.

"I get tired," I croaked.

"When they going to let you out then?"

"Three days' time. Hard to believe, but that's what the nurse said today."

"You bin in the wars," he said. "You got to rest."

An image of the world at rest on a beach flashed into my mind, epic regiments of sunbathers like those terracotta soldiers from China—but lying down of course instead of standing up.

"We're on our holidays!" I said, with a great big smile.

I felt outstandingly happy; I felt like I was floating.

"That's right, mate," he said. "We're on the Costa Brava. Hur-hur-hur."

"Don't make me laugh," I begged.

Part of me was horror-struck in case my wound opened up and my heart fell out. More, though, I was happy in a very basic way. These hospital beds weren't exactly padded sun-loungers but on the other hand they were definitely above ground rather than below it.

"Torremolinos!" said the man in the next bed. "Hur-hur-hur."

"Give it a rest," I pleaded, holding my sides and laughing very carefully.

EREWHON

03:29

Foolishly he had opened his eyes, and that was the time. Under four hours. He'd never get back. The straight-sided digits floated, gloated, lime green in the dark. That was tomorrow shot. Meanwhile Ella snored on beside him, oblivious.

Within ten seconds he was as wide awake as she was deep asleep. No, they hadn't started out like this but this was life now. What she couldn't seem to understand was that it was hard, he found it very hard to run the house and look after her and the children as well as hold down a full-time job. It surprised him—embarrassed him, even—that she couldn't seem to see this for herself. Didn't she care? If he said anything though she got angry and walked out of the room.

03:32

Think about something else. The Performance Management Review coming up at school next week. Another teaching hoop to jump through. His line manager would be observing him formally and every single one of his students would need to be seen as having made exceptional progress during the observed lesson for him to get an Outstanding. He was breaking into a light sweat just thinking about it.

He wanted to go part-time. That was what he was nerving himself up for. Dave Sweetland had agreed to a job-share if they could get it past the head. Part-time would mean he'd be able to cook something other than pasta and help Colin more with his homework and generally keep an eye on him—he was worried about him—as well as do boring but necessary things like sort out the boiler and take Daisy to the dentist and get his marking done before midnight. It would make all the difference. But he would have to be careful how he approached Ella.

It was so hard. If he got the wrong tone of voice she shouted and refused to listen. It was like treading on eggshells. Feminine pride. He'd have to present it to her as her own idea, that's what he'd have to do. If he could somehow show her that her life too would be improved by it, then it might work.

He cringed now, turning onto his right side, and curled into a foetal position. Whenever he said anything, she started talking about certain men at the hospital where she was director of facilities, working fathers who managed to do it all effortlessly and without fuss.

She'd say, Money. But he was going to get ill otherwise.

03:37

Stop worrying. Count backwards from a thousand. Nine hundred and ninety-nine. That was another good worry, whether he'd done the right thing not to report what he'd been told at the last parents' evening. Timothy Tisdall's father had sat opposite him for the obligatory four minutes and with tear-filled eyes had whispered to him what he suffered at the hands of his wife; how his wife was a policewoman so knew not to hit him anywhere it would show; how he couldn't report it and was begging him not to report it but how he had to tell someone and thank you for listening, it made him feel less alone.

There was bit of pushing and shoving sometimes from Ella, but she didn't hit him. Nine hundred and ninety-eight. Not nice to think how the overwhelming majority of men who were murdered were murdered by their own wives.

03:41

He'd better stock up on whisky. Ella's mother was the next blot on the horizon. A bombastic, hard-drinking woman in her mid-sixties, she had recently divorced her long-suffering second husband and replaced him with a trainee barista a third her age. They were coming to lunch at the weekend and he was thinking of pasta; he was simply too busy and tired for anything else but Ella wouldn't be pleased.

It was hard, the way older women got better with age while men lost their sexual allure. It was an unfair fact of nature. Our skin is so much coarser, he reflected, prone to early furrows and open pores and sag; and then of course—unfairest of all—we go bald. Nobody really respects a man anymore once he turns forty, particularly if he's losing it on top.

03:48

And the media is so disparaging of men over forty, he thought; the way it zooms in on our paunches and spindle shanks, our pendulous earlobes. Another real worry was, he was developing turkey wattles. Ella had noticed it too—she'd called him jowly the other day, she'd pinched an incipient fold of flab while ostensibly chucking him under the chin.

Why can't there be some positive older role models for a change, he fretted. Wherever you went, images of young men in next to nothing were in your face, making you feel bad about your body. His route to work was tyrannised by giant posters of ripped abs, honed six-packs, buff biceps.

In a pathetic attempt to fight back, he'd recently been engaging in a spot of newsagent guerrilla warfare. Now when he bought his paper he made sure to stick some of his prepared Post-it notes to the naked boys on the covers of the women's magazines—notes he had felt-tipped in advance with the words WHAT IF HE WAS YOUR SON?

03:50

Moving deeper into the forest of worries, his mind now fixed on Colin's silence and pallor. He'd shown signs of shaky self-esteem from early on, his boy Colin, and now, at the age of thirteen, it seemed he might be flirting with anorexia. There was the other thing too, which was even more worrying, the cutting thing; but he wasn't going to mention that to Ella yet.

Whereas Daisy, at nine, knew exactly what she wanted and it definitely didn't involve self-excoriation. She was obsessed, already, with the most brainless computer games, all about domination and detonation. She needed ferrying round for miles at weekends for her competitive yoga, which she was taking to County level—there was talk of trials in Birmingham, Ella was very thrilled. Not that he resented this for a moment; he was proud of her too, of course he was, and he was able to get on with his marking while he waited outside various sports venues for the necessary hours. But it would have been nice to get a thank-you once in a while.

He really must stop bleating.

What a loser! No wonder Colin's self-esteem was low with *him* as a role model.

Was he managing to be a good father to him? That was what really worried him—him and the other dads. They all agonised endlessly about whether or not they were good fathers.

04:04

His heart was very slow, wasn't it? It felt like it was labouring up a hill. Thump. Thump. Thump.

Now it was racing! Something must be wrong. He wasn't overjoyed about still being on the Pill.

All four of his grandparents had died of strokes or heart attacks, but Ella couldn't tolerate condoms. They muffled things, she said.

04:08

While he was getting undressed last night she'd had the cheek to say, "Those pants are getting tired."

"They're not the only ones!" he'd flashed back, the worm turning, keenly aware that it wasn't just his pants that were being criticised.

Afterwards she had rolled off him and fallen asleep with a snore.

04:13

He knew he really should think about his own satisfaction as well but somehow it was so much easier at the time to concentrate on gauging her levels of interest and to adapt himself to what worked for her. The trouble was, he himself needed some patience and encouragement, he found it really didn't work for him without at least five minutes' foreplay.

"Oh for God's sake, get it up and get on with it," she'd snapped at him the other night—though, to give her her due, she had apologised soon afterwards. Still, he couldn't help resenting her impersonal demands for sex; her obdurate refusal to talk, ever. Then there were her smothered belches, the semi-stifled farts she seemed to find so hilarious, not to mention the mulch of underwear she left in her wake or the state she left the bathroom in on a nightly basis. It was like the stables at the end of the world once she'd finished with it.

04:21

A bird had started up outside, and light was looming round the edges of the curtains. He closed his eyes without much hope and began to count apples on an imaginary tree.

04:22

No, that was no good. Try the one which made him tired just to think about, the one where he was climbing the steps of a spiral staircase which he saw was endless.

He knew Ella watched porn online. That was why she was so late coming to bed—"Just checking my emails." She didn't know he knew and he wasn't going to tell her, but there was the evidence on her laptop when he tapped into it—Loaded Lunchbox, Bollocks 'n' Bunfights, all those fit and perfect men.

He understood the arguments: it's completely mainstream; everybody looks at porn; it's just another way of relaxing. But something in him protested against it.

"Don't be such a MascuNazi," Ella said if he ever said anything. He hated it when she called him that. But it's important that we get more men out of prostitution, he'd been saying; that we get more men into Parliament. "Of course it is, darling," she'd replied indulgently.

To be fair, she did sometimes listen to him rant on about the injustice of the system. She even agreed with what he said, which was after all based on facts, incontrovertible. But she had no interest in changing it. Why would she when it worked so well for her?

04:30

He could see how he had to come last in the family pecking order. Something had to give and it wasn't going to be Ella. And he couldn't bear it to be the children.

He minded that she rode over him roughshod, that she made all the big decisions, the ones about money and hours, without consulting him. The last thing he wanted was to be accused of being shrill, though, and anything he said to contradict her did not go down well at all.

04:33

It all made him feel rather depressed. Which accounted for the chocolate he squirrelled away round the house. A good woman is hard to find, he was in the habit of reminding himself as he broke off another row of Fruit & Nut. This didn't help shrink his paunch one bit, but he had to have something.

04:42

"Is it just that women aren't as nice as men?" he'd blurted out at the last book club meeting.

"They're certainly more ruthless than us," Mike had said, looking pensively at his fingernails. "The real difference seems to be that they're able to compartmentalise. They can cut off. And of course they're more ambitious."

"I'd be ambitious too if it was allowed!" Dave had laughed.

They had all laughed at that.

"It's the famous old triple conundrum," Dave had continued. "You can have two out of three but not three. You can have the woman and the job, or the woman and the children. But you can't have the woman *and* the job *and* the children."

"Why not?" he'd persisted. "*Women* don't have to choose! Why can they have it all and not us?"

"That's life," Dave had shrugged.

05:11

It was about power, really, in the end—but he'd never thought of himself as a political person. Ella wouldn't talk about it. She wouldn't put herself out to talk to him, or to listen to him either. "Childcare?" she'd yawn if he asked her for a couple of hours off. "That's your job. Just do it!" She'd say it in an ironical way—obviously!—but even so he'd find it difficult to laugh. She was big on irony; she frequently got irony to do her dirty work for her. Then she'd accuse him of being humourless.

He could feel rage bubbling up in spite of himself.

"You're so *angry*," she'd chided last time he'd complained. "It's very unattractive."

05:20

He was holding the lime-green digits in view, and gave a little moan as they flicked to 05:21. He had been stretched over this mental gridiron for what felt like hours, tossing and turning until he was scorched on all sides. No chance of sleep now. Ella was snoring away beside him on her unassailable barge of slumber. Rage swept through him. YES he was angry! Here he was, lying in bed worrying, scrolling back through the week wondering what steps he could take to improve things between them; and here she was, impervious, complacent, sleeping like Queen Log.

Surely she should make an effort too? If she loved him? Didn't she see how unfair it all was? Surely she'd noticed how his vitality had had to be progressively tamped down, year on year, since the arrival of their first child? This unilateral decision to preserve her life in its pristine state within their marriage—untrammelled by domestic duties or family admin—when had it been taken? How had he been persuaded into colluding?

Well, it was either that or leave. *She* wasn't going to give an inch.

He loved her, he wanted her respect. He knew she loved him too, really; what puzzled him was how she could be happy to exploit him in such a blatantly unequal setup.

"I know you'll do things if I nag for long enough,"

he'd said to her on their last holiday. "What I really want, though, is for you to take on some of the worrying. Some of the actual work, the thinking and feeling."

"But I know you'll do that for me." She'd smiled. And she'd been right.

So it was generally agreed that men were nicer than women, less selfish, more caring; men had been awarded the moral high ground. Big deal! And was that supposed to make everything all right? He twisted in the dark, the acid reflux of injustice rising in him. The world wasn't going to change just because he wanted it to, though, was it. The world was woman-shaped—get over it!

07:10

When he woke up, everything was exactly the same as it had been the night before. Of course it was; unimaginable that it wouldn't have been. And there would be absolutely no point in dragging any of these night thoughts up into the daylight, he decided as he drew the curtains; nothing was going to change. This was the way things were. This was the natural order.

KENTISH TOWN

"What can I say," said Nancy, "but, sorry. *The Chimes* was my choice. I remembered it from a story tape years ago in the car and all I can say is, it was better that way."

"Yes," said Estella. "I almost gave up after that unbelievably boring long-winded first sentence. Though by the end I was glad I'd stuck with it."

"Oh good," said Nancy. "The thing is, it needs to be read aloud. It needs an actor, a really gravelly strong voice and lots of hammy emphasis."

"Sorry, I haven't read it," said Dora. "Let alone had it read to me. I've been doubling up for one of the other GPs in the practice who's been off sick then the moment my head hits the pillow I'm out like a light."

The three of them were sitting round Nancy's kitchen table in Kentish Town. It was the last book group meeting of the year, and they were two down (Nell had flu, Lizzie's father had broken his hip), while Rashmi had just texted to say she'd been held up at work but hoped to come on later.

"Have you got a banana?" asked Dora. "I'm starving, I've come straight from the surgery."

"You should have cancelled," said Nancy, reaching for the fruit bowl. "You must be exhausted."

"Cancel?" said Dora. "No chance. If I'd gone home I'd have had to cook for them all. And I wanted to see *you*! This must be the best value night out there is, meeting old friends somewhere warm that doesn't cost money or need booking in advance, out of the wind and rain."

Their book group was of the kind only possible in a big city where individual members need not impinge on each other's worlds socially. They knew and trusted each other well enough from their monthly meetings over the years to be able to speak with a frankness that couldn't be afforded elsewhere. Indeed, they knew rather too much about each other now to be able to bring their respective families together for any length of time.

"Here's to old friends," said Nancy, pouring more wine. "And here's to the Tackleton Road School gates too all those years ago, without which we might never have met. Would you like some nuts and raisins, Dora? Toast? Cheese? I broke up last Friday and I'm not going to touch my marking till January so I'm all right; but you must be extra busy with all the seasonal viruses. When do you stop?"

"Christmas Eve," said Dora.

"Me too," said Estella. "*And* I've got the dreaded office party tomorrow night."

"I can't say I feel that much sympathy," said Nancy. "A party in a newspaper office has got to be more glamorous than warm white wine in polystyrene cups in the staff room. You probably wear cocktail dresses!"

"Like hell we do," said Estella. "That was my last coup, by the way, five hundred words in forty-three minutes flat: how to survive the office party. Don't drink too much, don't sit on the photocopier, wear a sparkly hair-slide. 'Tis the season to churn out the same old stuff as last year and the year before and the year before *that*."

"Bah humbug," said Dora, laughing. "That's what Christmas is *about*, Estella, that's what people want—for it to be the same! It's reassuring, the tree and the turkey and something Dickensy on in the background."

"Don't even mention that man's name," growled Estella. "It's all his fault, Christmas. This week I've had to do a round-up of the latest Scrooge-themed stocking-fillers *and* write a piece about how the great writer dumped his wife complete with quotes from some Harley Street doctor pronouncing on the male menopause."

"The main reason I chose *The Chimes*, of course," said Nancy, "was to avoid *A Christmas Carol*. Someone said they wanted something Christmassy to read in December . . ."

"Not me," said Estella.

"No, Lizzie, I think it was; and when I suggested M. R. James, Nell said she was spooked by ghost stories. But I simply couldn't face Scrooge in his nightgown and Marley's wretched door knocker all over again, having taught it three years running to Year Ten on the basis that it's one of the shortest on the list and some of them might actually get to the end of it."

"That was the best thing about *The Chimes*," said Estella. "It was short. Eighty pages."

". . . and what it really boils down to, *A Christmas Carol*, is: buy a turkey, save your soul," said Nancy. "Whereas *The Chimes* has got alcoholism and prostitution and all sorts of topical issues."

"Ding dong," sang out Dora.

"That must be Rashmi," said Nancy, getting up from the table. "Help yourselves to wine."

Rashmi had come in a black cab straight from Canary Wharf.

"Great shoes," said Estella, once the round of kissing was over.

"I only wear them because I have to," said Rashmi. "It's because I'm five-two without them and the guys I work with are patronising enough as it is—I don't want them patting me on the head too."

"I simply couldn't get through the day if I had to wear heels," said Nancy. "Like air hostesses in the old days. I'd be in agony."

"You have to be tiny if you're going to wear stilettos," said Estella. "Nearer eight stone than nine. I know these things, I've done a feature on them, it's all to do with centre of gravity and pressure per square centimetre."

"That reminds me, I've got some mince pies waiting," said Nancy, turning the oven on.

"I hope you went ahead without me," said Rashmi. "I haven't read the book, it's been round the clock at work."

"Right, that's fifty-fifty," said Estella. "Nancy and I have both read it, you and Dora haven't had time, so why don't we get Nancy to go into teacher mode and tell you two what it was all about, with the odd ad lib from me?"

"Sounds good," said Rashmi, taking a large sip of wine and slipping off her shoes.

"He had a smash hit with *A Christmas Carol* when he was thirty-one," said Nancy, "and he wrote *The Chimes* the following year to capitalise on this success. He had whole roomfuls of people sobbing when he read it to them. But even his very first novel, *The Pickwick Papers,* has all those festive scenes in Dingley Dell and he wrote that when he was only twenty-four, so he was obviously mad on Christmas from the start."

"Abnormal," said Estella.

"Pickwick," said Rashmi, "that's the one on the Quality Street tin, right? The little fat guy?"

"Oh when my boy Ollie was two I used to call him Mr. Pickwick," said Dora. "Stumping round on his stout little legs and a great big smile on his face. Not that I ever read it."

"You don't need to, really," said Estella. "It's just there, isn't it, like Shakespeare. To be or not to be. Please, sir, I want some more. Same sort of thing."

"Anyway," said Nancy. "Back to *The Chimes*. Instead of the Ghost of Christmas Past we have the Spirits of the Bells ringing out various New Year messages. Because it's not actually Christmas in *The Chimes* but New Year's Eve."

"New Year's Eve," said Estella. "That's another bummer."

"It's certainly the busiest night of the year in Casualty," said Dora. "I was on A&E at the Whittington one New Year's Eve, and in that single night I remember putting in six chest lines! There were more knife wounds and fractured skulls than you could shake a stick at. People staggering in from the pubs dripping with blood, still fighting quite often, it was pure mayhem."

"Lovely," said Nancy. "Meanwhile, let's meet our hero, Trotty Veck. He's a London ticket porter. That was a sort of porter-cum-postman at the time—I looked it up—wearing a white apron and a licence badge and basically he would stand around by the church in all weathers waiting to run errands for small change."

"Yes, it's good on him being cold and rained on," said Estella. "Trotty keeps warm by trotting everywhere rather than walking. Hence the name."

"I suppose the modern equivalent would be a motorbike courier," said Rashmi.

"But everybody who wasn't rich would have walked then," said Nancy. "Bob Cratchit lived in Camden and he walked into the City every day to Scrooge's office; that's what the clerks did, thousands of them from all the London suburbs, still half-awake, trudging off to work in the early morning."

"It must have been a bit like it was after the bombs on

the Underground," said Estella. "Thousands of us plodding along in silence together. Hardly any traffic; weirdly quiet. It was so strange."

"He was a great walker himself, Dickens," said Nancy. "A steady four miles per hour, he needed it to let off steam. When he was writing he used to get so excited in his imagination that he'd have to tramp the London streets fifteen to twenty miles a night to calm down."

"Twenty?" said Estella. "Are you *sure*? That would be, let's see, five hours straight without any rests."

"I'd better read this book, I think," said Rashmi. "He sounds quite a dynamo. In Mumbai, by the way, the clerks come in to work by train from the suburbs while their wives spend the morning preparing various little fresh dishes for their lunch. Then each clerk's lunch is packed in stacking tins and collected by a man on a bicycle—another version of your Trotty Veck, it sounds like—but this bicycle man is called a tiffin-wallah. And there are thousands of them too, the tiffin-wallahs, all cycling like mad delivering individual wife-cooked lunches to the clerks every day."

"How amazing!" said Dora in delight. "Imagine having home-cooked food every day! I just grab what I can on the run—I'm not fussy, sandwich, Mars Bar . . ."

"Banana," said Estella.

"Banana!" said Dora, laughing.

"Better than Trotty got," said Estella. "That's what happens next: it's cold and rainy and Trotty's daughter brings him some hot lunch in a basket. And it's tripe."

"Oh, surely not!" said Dora. "It is Dickens, after all."

"No, no, the food in the basket is tripe! Stewed tripe."

"The stomach of a cow," said Rashmi. "They've started putting it back on the menu at some of the restaurants in the City."

She wrinkled her nose and took a sip of wine.

"My grandmother used to make it," said Estella. "Lots of onions. *She* read Dickens. Not much else except the *Mirror* and the *People's Friend,* no other books in the house, but she did read Dickens. When I tried him once there, as a child, I said he was boring and she said, At least he wasn't a snob."

"Anyway, nothing to do with the tripe, but Trotty's been getting a bit existential," said Nancy. "He's over sixty and he's started wondering whether he even has the right to be alive if he's poor and in debt. Let me see, where is that bit—I've marked it—here it is, about the poor. 'I can't make out whether we have any business on the face of the earth, or not. Sometimes I think we must have—a little; and sometimes I think we must be intruding,' he says. 'We seem to be dreadful things; we seem to give a deal of trouble; we are always being complained of and guarded against. One way or other, we fill the papers.'"

"Yes, that's a good bit," said Estella. "*Faux naïf* but in a good way. And that's why the Spirits of the Bells visit him in the form of visions, to reproach him for not being more positive."

"*The Chimes* is all about how the rich don't give a stuff about the poor, basically," said Nancy. "Dickens could see there was hunger and squalor everywhere in London; he could hear and read about it in the rest of the country, how children under seven were being put to work in the mills, the mines, for up to twelve hours a day; and he was outraged."

"In India," said Rashmi, "there are literally millions of bonded child labourers working twelve-hour days to pay off their parents' debts. It's a scandal but it goes on."

"Not that there isn't poverty here anymore," said Dora. "There is. You should see how some of my patients have to live. But it's relative, isn't it."

"Yes," said Rashmi. "It is."

Estella dipped her head as if to stifle an incipient yawn.

"On with the story," said Nancy. "Trotty's daughter Meg wants to marry her intended, a strapping virtuous labourer, on New Year's Day; but two random rich men—Alderman Cute and Mr. Filer—advise her against this. They tell her she hasn't got enough money to get married and would only have children who went wrong and a husband who left her destitute and herself be driven to ruin and suicide. The two rich men are quite funny because they're so awful, going on and on about the good old times, the good old times, and being incredibly patronising to Trotty and Meg about the tripe dinner as well as everything else."

"So what does Dickens suggest?" asked Rashmi. "A revolution?"

"There is that cardboard character, Will Fern, isn't there, Nancy, a bit later on," said Estella. "Another noble workman maddened by the Poor Laws and the rest of it. Near the end *he's* threatening to go off and set fire to things."

"Yes," said Nancy. "But Dickens isn't a revolutionary. Not the guillotine sort, anyway. No. He wants . . . a change of heart. He wants the people with lots of money to start minding about the people with not enough money."

"Yes, that would be nice," said Dora.

"Scrooge gives the Cratchits a turkey?" said Rashmi.

"Exactly," said Nancy. "Philanthropy. And that's what we're being shunted back towards now. I can't believe it. We had a perfectly good welfare state; the eighth wonder of the world, it was, far more impressive than putting men on the moon. Personally I think we knocked the Americans into a cocked hat when we invented the welfare state."

"Nancy," said Estella.

"For a society to reach the point," said Nancy, "where it considers its less fortunate or able members, and via taxation keeps them from starvation and homelessness and all the worst terrors of poverty—what a triumph! What dignity in it! Our parents were proud of it. *Their* parents, who lived through the thirties, could hardly believe it. Even *I* remember regarding the state as my friend when I was at university because it was paying for me to be there, though it wasn't fashionable to say so at the time. And now it's all being dismantled and run into the ground and we're being told to suck up to sponsors instead."

"Nancy!" said Rashmi.

"No," said Nancy, "we're being sent back to the world of forelock-tugging and thank'ee kindly, sir. It seems so . . . Victorian. We're not American, we're not used to the idea of starting a college fund the minute we have a baby. We just don't have that tradition, even if *they* never got beyond it."

"Nancy?" said Dora.

"We had free university education for the first time and assumed it would be the same for our children," continued Nancy, "particularly since the country had got so much richer in the interim. But no, the money we thought we were saving for our old age must now go to our children instead. And as for them, our children, they're spending their vacations chugging the streets to help fund themselves through college. Chugging! That's rich."

"Phew," said Estella.

"Hmm," said Rashmi.

Nancy poured herself a glass of water.

"What's chugging?" said Dora.

"Charity mugging," said Nancy. "You know, when you're collared on the street by a bright young man looking you in the eye and asking you to sign up for a standing order. Oh, I know, and it's obviously nice when some billionaire wants to do good once they've got too much and can't think what else to do with it—but surely it would be better if the system wasn't arranged so that certain individuals can grab a great pile for themselves by exploiting everybody else in the first place?"

"What—capitalism?" said Rashmi. "But you do know, Nancy, don't you? Capitalism has won. It's the best—well, the least bad system."

"I thought that was democracy," said Estella. "The least bad system."

"Well, neither of them seems to be working very well at the moment," said Nancy.

"It's not that simple," said Rashmi.

"It is that simple," said Nancy.

"It is and it isn't," said Dora.

"Glad we've got *that* sorted out," said Estella.

"In fact, it's all gone berserk," continued Nancy. "I've never been on strike before, but I did join in recently. Because it's not fair. It's not *fair*."

"Can we get back to *The Chimes*?" said Rashmi. "I was hoping to work up a bit of Christmas spirit this evening."

"And as for the riots, well, riots aren't logical, are they," said Nancy. "They're emotional."

"Nancy," said Estella. "Have a mince pie."

"Yes," said Rashmi. "Shush."

"Sorry," said Nancy. "Steam coming out of my ears."

"Completely understandable," said Dora. "I sympathise."

"Let's get back to Trotty Veck and his daughter Meg," said Estella. "Meg. Oh dear, oh dear, Meg. It's true what they say, Dickens couldn't do women. Not women between fifteen and thirty, anyway. They're nothing but passive characterless stooges, his young female characters.

And in fact it's only just coming out now, what he was like with the real women in his life."

"What *was* he like?" said Dora.

"Total nightmare," said Estella. "I read all about it for that menopause feature I was telling you about. When he married Catherine what's-her-name she was twenty, he wasn't much older, and he made it clear from the start that he wanted a wife who would never contradict or question him and who would always do what he said. OK, he was a genius, they're allowed to be control freaks. But then, when she'd had ten children not counting the miscarriages he decided she was boring—which she probably was after all that—plus, he was seeing an eighteen-year-old actress."

"Not an unusual story," said Rashmi. "What we call it now is trading in the wife for a younger model, surely."

"Yes, but it was worse than that," said Estella. "Because he wanted the moral high ground as well as to be shot of his boring wife. So he exiled her, he sent her away. He bad-mouthed her to all his friends and even to the press—he was a famous man by then—saying she was a bad mother who didn't love her children, and her children didn't love her, and that she was generally mad and jealous and unhinged. The law meant the children were his property of course, and he discouraged them from seeing or speaking to her. It was the cruellest thing you can think of."

"How could he *do* that?" cried Dora.

"It was deeply hysterical behaviour," said Estella. "Doesn't mean he wasn't a genius; but still. Can you imagine what that first Christmas without her must have been like, with their children not daring to mention her name? He must have somehow convinced himself that *he* was the injured party."

"It sounds very like Leo," said Rashmi. "Five years ago this Christmas. You remember?"

The rest of them nodded and looked solemn. Several years ago, Rashmi had made them party to the unfolding bitterness of her divorce and subsequent custody battle. The quasi-formal monthly appointment system of the book group meant that it had become a serial narrative to them, with increasingly melodramatic instalments. Her eyes glittered now with unshed tears as she poured herself some more wine.

"And yet, and yet," said Nancy, tactfully diverting attention from her. "It's not so simple. It never is, is it. Dickens could also be a friend to women, capable of deep sympathy and understanding. I was reading about it, and for several years, very discreetly, he helped Miss Coutts, a philanthropic heiress, to run a home in Shepherd's Bush for girls who'd gone wrong, providing them with a way to make new lives."

"Miss Coutts as in . . . ?" said Rashmi.

"Yes! Banking again!" said Nancy. "No, don't look like that, I won't start ranting; but I must just read you this bit from *The Chimes*—Sir Joseph Bowley's thoughts on the

New Year and bankers. Let me see; ah, here it is: '. . . at this season of the year we should think of—of—ourselves. We should look into our—our accounts. We should feel that every return of so eventful a period in human transactions, involves a matter of deep moment between a man and his—and his banker.'"

"Yes, that bit made me laugh too," said Estella, smiling broadly.

"I look around me at work and I see some very average people who've made a great deal of money over the last twenty years," said Rashmi, blowing her nose. "Second homes are the norm; I've got a flat in Mumbai so I shouldn't talk. But there are people with third homes, strings of rental properties, and they're nothing special in the way of ability or talent. We've lived through a time when it was perfectly possible to go from mediocre to millionaire as long as you had some energy and luck and an eye to the main chance."

"At least this lot today didn't inherit it," said Estella. "Not all of them, anyway."

"True," said Rashmi. "My boss's mother was a dinner lady."

"And that ought to make it better," said Nancy, "but somehow it doesn't. Once someone gets rich, it seems they immediately forget what it was like to be not rich. They just morph into money without a backward glance."

"Of course, the City always did do itself well," said Rashmi. "But over the last couple of decades it's quite obvious that it massively overrewarded itself."

"Not 'arf, you haven't," said Estella. "You artful dodgers, you."

"But then since the turn of the century millions and millions of people have grown richer all over the world," said Rashmi, "particularly in India and China. The world's wealth has almost doubled."

"How?" said Dora. "How can the money in the world increase itself? Surely there's a finite amount? Doesn't make sense."

"It must be to do with the dicing and splicing and sub-priming we keep hearing about," said Nancy.

"I know," said Dora. "I try and follow it on the news, but honestly, it's beyond me."

"What I think," fumed Nancy, "is that never again can we afford to be so ignorant. We've allowed a pack of shameless greed-merchants and a few brainiacs with maths PhDs to rig the entire system over the last twenty years so that nobody can understand it. We must lobby for basic economics to be a compulsory part of the national curriculum from now on."

"I'm not sure how much good that would do," said Estella. "Even if we get the hang of what a hedge fund is, what securitisation means, so what? It's all got so complicated apparently that nobody in banking really understands it either. The only thing that's clear is, they're protected from their own mistakes."

"And Muggins pays," says Dora. "That's us."

"What would Dickens say?" said Nancy.

"If he had any sense," said Rashmi, "he would point

out that the average Brit may be feeling the pinch just now but they're still ten times richer than the average Chinese. And he would probably set his next Christmas story in Shenzhen or Dongguan, in a toy factory. He'd tell the story of a factory worker who lives twelve hours from where her small children are cared for by her parents while she works for a pittance and sleeps in a comfortless dormitory and only sees them once a year."

"Once a year!" said Dora. "That's not true, is it?"

"At Chinese New Year," said Rashmi. "Imagine those few days."

"Would it help if we didn't buy the toys?" asked Nancy.

"Not really," said Rashmi. "It's hard to beat a global system. There are people a lot worse off than our factory worker, and anyway she'd probably rather have the life she's got now than the one her mother's had. She's already richer than her parents ever were."

"We've all been part of our generation," said Nancy abruptly, "whether or not we've made any money. And I for one am ashamed of it. It's all of us that have done this. The lack of principle."

"What principle?" asked Rashmi. "Debt is bad?"

"Partly that, yes. At a very basic, Mr. Micawber level. But more, we haven't kept in mind what's fair, what's right. The governments we've elected have been shallow and greedy and now, it emerges, incompetent too."

"Harsh words," said Rashmi.

"Harsh facts," said Nancy. "Anyway, it looks like it's over now. We've had our turn."

There was a pause.

"OK. Setting the world to rights," said Nancy. "What have we come up with?"

"Pay people properly," said Estella.

"Don't switch off," said Dora. "Dickens was right—have sympathy for those with hard lives."

"Force through global financial regulation and make sure the rich pay their taxes," said Rashmi.

"Let's impose stringent global climate-control measures, too," said Nancy.

There was another pause.

"Right," said Estella. "That should do it."

The four of them clinked glasses and sipped the last of the wine.

"So how does it finish, *The Chimes*?" asked Dora.

"It's a bit of a cop-out, really," said Nancy. "Trotty wakes up and finds it was all just a dream."

"You're right," said Estella. "It gets rather huddled on to the last couple of pages, the ending. Meg gets married, someone else called Mrs. Chickenstalker who runs the corner shop discovers a long-lost something-or-other. They all wish each other happy New Year. And that's about it. Even so, as I said, I'm glad I read it."

"Me too," said Nancy. "Though I must say, I still prefer it read aloud. Now, diaries. How's January looking? Next time we meet we'll have left the old year behind. Any New Year's resolutions here?"

"Take less exercise," said Estella. "Put on half a stone."

"Well, actually, I thought I might try walking like Dickens," said Dora. "Fast, four miles an hour, at night, after work, for the two miles home. A very good way to let off steam."

"I'm going to read more about the way the world works," said Nancy.

"And I'm going to read more fiction," said Rashmi.

KYTHERA

EGGS, BUTTER, SUGAR, FLOUR; A LEMON. PREHEAT THE OVEN TO 180 DEGREES. And because as you know it's the one I always make, darling girl, I have the Lemon Drizzle recipe pretty much by heart. I wonder how many it is I've made for you and your brother over the years. If I tot up your joint ages and then throw in another twenty-odd for your father, that comes to, oh, more than sixty cakes between you. Yes.

MEASURE OUT FOUR OUNCES OF BUTTER AND FOUR OUNCES OF CASTER SUGAR FROM THE JAR WITH THE BLACK VANILLA POD. Do you remember when my cousin Hilary got me to help her make memory boxes for the children? Three of them, all under ten at the point when she heard it was terminal. Anyway, I shopped for three little bottles of her favourite scent, helped her choose photos of various high points in her life, that sort of thing. Poor Hilary. She was memorialising herself for them.

But when I told you and your brother about it—you weren't very old then either, just tiddlers—I was very struck by what you said. You both said you'd rather have the mum's memories of *you* as babies and funny things you said and did and things like that, with photos of her holding you or beaming at you, than a box just about *her.* And I thought, of course. Yes. Of course you would.

SIFT SIX OUNCES OF FLOUR WITH A TEASPOON OF BAKING POWDER. When I was expecting you I imagined you might be born on Midsummer's Eve because the ETA we'd been given was the fifteenth of June, which is near enough. But as it turned out that beautiful hot flower-filled summer you were late, weren't you; you didn't arrive until the first of July.

You were a perfect, calm, alert baby girl. I was amazed, after the protracted drama and violence of your two-day journey, broken collarbone and all, at how composed you were. Seven and a half pounds. They laid you in the glass hospital cot on your side and when I met your blue eyes—that dark newborn blue like Delft china—I was amazed. You knew me!

When we got home there was a bank of flowers, more than I've seen in my life before or since—roses and lilies and larkspur from all our friends, every jug and mug full of carnations and white daisies. That's why I still fill the kitchen with flowers in your birthday week—they're all in season, and I bake your cake surrounded by them.

At first you lay quietly in your Moses basket. Asleep, you played a silent flute, graceful long curling fingers up near your sweet face, eyes closed, lips parted to pout out a little purse of air. Oh you smelt delicious, I couldn't resist stroking your forehead with my nose, sniffing up your fabulous innocent smell. It was like clean washing and fresh gardens. Once you were here I couldn't bear synthetic smells. I switched to unscented soap; I wanted you to know *my* smell too.

CREAM THE BUTTER AND SUGAR TOGETHER WITH A FORK. And you fed like a dream, you even let me read a book while you were feeding. Your dad used to call you a little milksop. I sampled a few drops of my own milk at one point, I remember, through curiosity, and it tasted fresh and slightly sweet with a faint vanilla scent like this sugar.

STIR IN THE EGGS AND BEAT UNTIL LIGHT AND FLUFFY. It was you who decided when you were ready to move on from a diet of milk and puréed baby mush. How funny, I can date it exactly, like Juliet's nurse—it was your dad's birthday, six months and three weeks on from yours, and we'd taken you out for lunch with us to a French-style brasserie for the first time. You were sitting beside me in a high chair. When I looked up from the menu of *moules frites* and *onglet à l'échalote,* I was just in time to see you grab a piece of baguette from the basket on the table. You went at it like a ravenous meerkat. I almost fell off my chair. We couldn't stop laughing, your dad and me. You always made us laugh even when you were little and you still do, with your showers of talk and mad-cat flights of fancy.

There was that time one summer I remember so clearly, when you and me and your brother were playing in the sea, jumping in the waves and shouting.

"Picasso!" you declared during a lull, floating on your back. "He's the one that cut off his ear."

"No he's not," I said.

"That was Matisse," said your brother, doggy-paddling away, looking to me for confirmation. "No, it was Van Gogh. Wasn't it, Mum. *Why* did he?"

"He was sad and mad," I replied.

"No, he did it to impress his girlfriend," you insisted, bobbing up and down. " 'See how much I love you, how I've suffered for you, I've sent you my ear.' Then she ate it."

"She did not!" I said, outraged.

"She did," you sparkled, nodding your head, dancing in the waves. "She cooked it in a frying pan, then she ate it."

We couldn't stop laughing, the three of us; we were spluttering and choking and falling about in the sea. Do you remember?

FOLD THE FLOUR INTO THE MIXTURE A LITTLE AT A TIME. I've got my grandmother's old cake tin ready by the scales, lined as she showed me with greaseproof paper snipped and fitted to size. That's where you got your lovely green eyes from, your great-grandmother. She used to make Seed cake in this tin, a very plain cake flavoured with half a teaspoon of caraway seeds. It was good and wholesome but more austere than we're used to now. When the cake was almost cooked she'd hold it up to her ear and listen to it—if it was singing away to itself inside, it needed longer. Whereas my mother's cakes—your grandma's—were altogether quicker and sweeter: a chocolate refrigerator cake packed with glacé cherries, or a Victoria sandwich with butter icing for our birthdays.

Then there was the time on that holiday in Kythera when all the younger children fell in love with you. You were eleven or maybe twelve. In the warm black evenings when there was music outside you became the Pied Piper—you had the adults clapping in time as you organised a miniature conga of children and got them dancing between the tables. You led them in triumph, the little girls gazing at you in a glory of adoration, and your brother and the other boys bouncing along in your wake with smiling spring-heeled obedience. And one-and-a-two-and-a-three-and-a-four, you all chanted as the music segued into the song that was so popular that summer, making rhythmic crisscross patterns with your arms: HEY! Macarena.

ZEST THE LEMON USING THE FINE SIDE OF THE GRATER, AND STIR INTO THE MIXTURE WITH TWO OR THREE TABLESPOONS OF MILK UNTIL IT REACHES A DROPPING CONSISTENCY. At your thirteenth birthday party you were luminously beautiful, as if lit from inside by candles, in a white dress with silver sparkles. We stood together at the front door to ward off gatecrashers. Almost all the still-almost-children arriving were nervous—the little flush high on their cheeks, the gabbled or absent greeting and a roll of the eyes like a startled horse. Then, half an hour in, they had acquired a cockiness, strutting round like pirates or arrogant nobles, high on the cushion of air lifting them off the ground in the generalised terror and desperation to be accepted and if possible to rule the roost, to dominate—to be a star. It was a night of high emotion—little trios and quartets of girls storming across rooms together or knotted into furious tête-à-têtes. The wordless boys got uppish and stroppy, jostling each other, showing off. Some of them tried to set fire to the garden shed; they were the ones who'd arrived together and presented you with three goldfish in a glass bowl. You were trembling with shock and excitement at the unavoidable immediacy of it, and your eyes met mine imploringly for a second as you took hold of their unwieldy offering.

SPOON THE MIXTURE INTO THE PREPARED TIN AND LEVEL OFF WITH A PALETTE KNIFE. When your next birthday loomed you said, "I can't believe I'm going to be fourteen next week. I'm going to post leaflets everywhere saying I'm available for light gardening." Then the fifteenth brought a slew of cards bursting with braggadocio about Bacardi Breezers, and *Almost Legal* scrawled naughtily across them. Chloë, Zoë, Lulu, Hannah, Scarlett—they all came back after school and sang heartily to you in the back garden over the candle-decked Lemon Drizzle; then the six of you scoffed several pounds of strawberries dipped in sugar. You wrote each other long birthday letters, rammed with the detail of shared lives and protestations of undying loyalty. "You're nothing to do with me," you told your mothers. "I only need you for lifts."

One morning when I went into your bedroom to wake you for school you looked up at me from your pillow with loathing and blurted, "I dreamt it was my birthday and you said, 'Now, darling, I've bought you a very special birthday present, and at first you may not think it's special but it is and it will teach you to be responsible. It's a flock of sheep; you'll need to look after them and remember to feed them and keep the gate shut and so on.'" From my position of weary maternal power I realised that overnight I had become your very own memento mori in bulging middle-aged shoes; your personal chaperone, duenna and spoilsport rolled into one nauseating bundle.

There followed showdowns in changing rooms and bust-ups on high streets; handles were flown off all over the place, and I started to feel quite glum; until, one day, ding! it dawned on me that it was nothing personal. It was just part of it, and a useful and necessary part of it at that. It wasn't me you couldn't stand: it was me-the-mother. Remember the story of Proteus in your favourite book of Greek myths? Well, you were like Proteus, the god of changeability, and my job was to hang on to you for dear life while you struggled against me, transforming yourself into a leopard, a snake, a pig, a bristling tree. I had to hold on to you, yes, but I also had to get off your back. That was the trick, the paradox. I'd say, "It's a lovely sunny day"; you'd say, "Don't tell me what to wear." Hold fast; back off! Freedom and security in a balance; closeness without intrusiveness. It's what we all want, and not just when we're young. Then, two or three birthdays ago, after the achievement of that necessary second separation, the weather picked up and we found ourselves to our mutual pleasure and relief united in once more agreeing that it was indeed a lovely sunny day.

SQUEEZE THE JUICE FROM THE ZESTED LEMON AND ADD IT TO FOUR OUNCES OF SUGAR. Strictly speaking this thin syrup is a version of glacé icing, but sharper and grittier. Poured over the cake while it's still warm from the oven it will form a translucent glaze, right at the other end of the scale from the showy tooth-deep pastel frosting on a cupcake. That seems to be the default career option for recent graduates now that the job market's imploded: set up a cupcake business from your mother's kitchen. No worse than languishing in some unpaid internship, I suppose; but talk about "let them eat cake."

Don't give up on politics, sweetheart; don't say nothing you do will make any difference. Things change. Hedged about as we are with snake-tongued bullies and greed-merchants, the main thing is to be brave and speak up. But what do I know. The heat of the changing world will act on you and you'll rise to it.

That rich, homely smell always surprises me. A tin of sticky raw ingredients goes into the oven and turns into something delicious that didn't exist before. It's very basic magic; and if I could wave a magic wand over the future I'd wish you luck, which everyone needs; and satisfying work that pays enough and allows you to look after your children too (if you have them) without half-killing yourself; and the love of a good man (or woman). Don't ever say yes, by the way, unless you like the way they smell. That's vital, along with integrity—but smell comes first.

Now. TAKE THE CAKE OUT OF THE OVEN. One of my best, though I say so myself. AND ALLOW IT TO COOL FOR A FEW MOMENTS BEFORE CAREFULLY TURNING IT ONTO A WIRE RACK. Perfect. PRICK ALL OVER WITH A FORK IN A CRISS-CROSS PATTERN, THEN POUR ON THE LEMON SYRUP WHILE THE CAKE IS STILL WARM. Mmm: delicious! *And* I've remembered the candles. Happy birthday, darling girl.

MOSCOW

Get my knee fixed then get the fridge-freezer fixed, that was the plan. I'd set everything up for a couple of days off on the basis that the medics had suggested a week. Might as well make myself useful, I thought; for once be the one to wait in for the repair man. God knows Nigel has had more than his fair share of it over the years—waiting in.

Don't run on it for six weeks, don't do this, don't do that; then the nurse was making me practise going up and down stairs with a stick for a good half-hour before the op. Waste of time! I was fine. The bruising was fairly dramatic, mustard-coloured below the knee—English mustard too, not French—and purple-black above. But it really didn't hurt that much.

The freezer man arrived right on time which I wasn't expecting, Nigel having warned me there was a less than fifty-fifty chance of this happening in his experience. Plain black T-shirt and jeans, close-cropped hair, he was rather short and very strongly built. Martial arts? I thought to myself.

"Water's dripping into the top salad drawer from somewhere and freezing hard," I told him. "Then it melts and freezes again."

I'd have gone away at this point and put in a few calls to work if it hadn't been for Nigel instructing me to stick with the process throughout. His reasoning was that it helped if you were able to explain to them what had gone wrong next time it happened, and the only way to understand what the problem was was to go through the whole boring process with them in the first place and ask questions and try to understand it. He himself took notes, dated, before he forgot; he had a special file for them. Nigel's an academic, he likes writing things down. His last published article was "Islamic Historians in Eighth- and Ninth-Century Mesopotamia and Their Approach to Historical Truth." I haven't read it yet but I know it'll be brilliant, like all his work. Anyway, I resigned myself to doing things his way this time, seeing as it was once in a blue moon that I was the one hanging around.

The man refused coffee when I offered but asked for a glass of water instead. All a bit of a novelty for me, this. I couldn't quite place his accent: East European, but not Polish.

He opened the door to the freezer compartment and our eating habits were laid bare. Sliced bread, because you can toast it from frozen; litre cartons of skimmed milk so we didn't ever run out; several tubs of ice cream (cookie dough for Georgia, mango and passion fruit for Verity, raspberry sorbet for weight-conscious Clio). Not much else except frozen peas and a bottle of vodka. Not much actual food. Oh well, everyone seemed healthy enough. The vodka was officially Georgia's now she was eighteen, for pre-drinking with her friends; better here where we could keep an eye on how fast it goes down, we'd reasoned, than hidden in her bedroom.

"So where are you from?" I asked, setting the glass of water down beside him.

He looked up from the fridge drawer for a moment. He had very dark eyes, like a watchful bird.

"Russia," he said.

Snow and ice, I thought; appropriate.

"Where in Russia?"

"Nearest city Moscow," he said; then, with fleeting mockery, "three hundred kilometres."

"So you're from the countryside?"

He nodded.

"I've been to Moscow," I said, but he'd turned back to the freezer.

That time I thought we might get into emerging markets, invest in commodities, get a piece of the action, I couldn't believe how long it took to get there. Not the flight but the actual drive from the airport into Moscow. The roads were atrocious; it took almost three hours in the cab for what should have been a forty-five-minute journey. The crawl through the gridlocked suburbs was teeth-grindingly slow. Then when I visited Mr. Petrossian in his office there were a couple of security guys with submachine guns in reception. The secretaries and support staff, all female of course, were trussed up in pencil skirts, tottering around on stilettos. It was like a surly version of the fifties. Embarrassing.

The man was lying spreadeagled on the floor now, shining a little torch into the gap beneath the freezer from which he'd neatly wrenched the grille. Seen from this angle it was obvious he worked out. I found myself wondering what sport he played and at what level.

I was going to go ballistic if I couldn't play tennis for six weeks. But of course that's what had done the damage in the first place—cartilage, wear and tear, fragments of cartilage which had broken off and were floating around in the synovial fluid. We'll just have a root-around, clear out the gunge, said the surgeon. He'd already done half a dozen that afternoon by the time he got to me, the nurse told me afterwards; a light general anaesthetic, just enough to put me under the surface for twenty minutes, then in at a nick beside the kneecap with his keyhole gizmo. I was all done by eight. I hadn't needed to drag Nigel out after all but had gone down in the lift and straight to the cab rank outside.

The cabbie asked me whether I had any children as we set off over the bridge and I said, as I always do when I'm asked this question, yes, three lovely daughters. If I say "stepdaughters" I find I get quizzed about whether I want my "own" children—and by complete strangers too. I adore the girls and that's been enough for me. Broody? Phases of it, in passing, like lust, and dealt with in the same way. Listen to your brain as well as the other stuff. Now, at fifty, I think I'm probably safe as well as fully occupied with running the business. It was shortlisted for the Dynamo Prize for Entrepreneurial Initiative last year.

Nigel was so sad when I met him. It *was* sad, being left a widower with three small children. Then after a while he wasn't sad anymore! He thinks I'm wonderful. He even loves my wonky nose—he says it's Roman; cartilage problems there too, that's next on the list. He thinks I'm beautiful though. He can't believe his luck, even now, twelve years on, bless him. Neither can I. The recipe for a happy marriage!

My mind was wandering all over the place. This was not like me; I was usually so focused. It must be some floaty postanaesthetic thing, I thought. Or maybe it was the unaccustomed feeling of having to do something that didn't interest me. I made an effort.

"What do you think the matter is then?" I asked, as the man sprang back noiselessly from a one-handed press-up. Impressive!

"First I check condenser coils," he said, selecting one from among his twenty or so screwdrivers.

"OK," I said, then added, "so do you miss Russia? The Russian countryside? Not much countryside near London."

"*Good* country near London," he said, turning to look at me.

"Really? Where's that then?"

"Brentwood."

"Brentwood?"

"Very good country," he repeated.

A smile flashed across his face before he could suppress it.

"Very good paintballing in Brentwood," he added.

That figured. I could just see him dodging from tree to tree with his paintball gun.

The one time I'd been inveigled into paintballing, while I was still at Renfrew's, it had been as part of some corporate team-bonding exercise. There were unflattering padded overalls to climb into, and a claustrophobic 360-degree helmet; also an uncomfortable neck guard to stop you getting shot in the throat. Paintball guns fire at surprisingly high velocity.

The objective had been to steal the other team's flag in a raid and bring it back to camp. At one point I'd been in possession of the flag. Returning to base, zigzagging to avoid the bullets as we'd been taught, gave me a weirdly nasty jacked-up feeling. I was running and I could see sudden blooms of colour bursting on the obstacles and trees in my sight line, turquoise and lime green and fluorescent yellow; every colour of the rainbow, except red of course. I got the flag back to our camp, we won the game, but I was still glad when it was over.

"It hurts," I said. "Paintballing."

"Some people shoot close range," he said, fiddling with his phone now. "Not good."

He showed me the phone screen and there was an anonymous torso sporting several big indigo bruises like starbursts.

"Ouch," I said, handing the phone back quickly. It felt like looking at porn. I didn't ask who it was; I didn't want to know.

Clio had brought back a paintballing invitation from school that term and I hadn't been sorry when it turned out a clash of dates meant she couldn't go.

Being a stepmother has been good in all sorts of ways. You're close, you love them, but there isn't quite the same cauldron of emotion. No, you can afford to get on with your work like anyone else.

I do earn more than Nigel of course. Considerably more. My business has gone from strength to strength in the last decade, while the terms of his university employment, his tenure and so on, have become increasingly insecure and ill-paid. He hasn't got as far up the academic greasy pole as he might have either, though he doesn't seem to mind. Maybe he'll write a surprise best-seller once he's retired, I tell him.

You're not supposed to say so but I'm very careful about employing women. This means in practical terms that I won't take on a woman who earns less than her partner. I need to be a hundred percent sure it's true of everyone on my payroll that *their* job comes first in the pecking order at home. No women with alpha-male husbands! I simply can't afford them.

Back to the freezer and apparently it wasn't the condenser coils after all.

"Next thing I test evaporator fan mechanism," he said, rooting round in his toolbox again.

"OK," I said, and started to make myself a coffee. "Another glass of water?"

He gave a quick nod.

Yes, funny the way that Russian trip worked out. Mr. Petrossian himself had been as clever and persuasive as when I'd met him at the trade fair in London, but there in Moscow he couldn't show me anything useful on paper about his business. He had to keep all the facts and figures in his head, he explained, as it wasn't a good idea to write things down. In the end we weren't able to strike a deal and I'm not particularly sorry looking back. Russia hasn't woken up yet. It's still only good for raw materials; it isn't actually making anything worth buying. No thanks, I thought, I'll stick with fibre optics.

Georgia locks horns with me about wicked capitalism now and then; she's doing politics, history, maths and economics A levels, clever girl, so it's good to hear the arguments. Liberal capitalism in the UK and the States has produced shocking inequality, she rages; regulation is toothless and it's getting worse not better. Correct, I say. Germany is the way to go, she says: corporate capitalism, more equality and a workforce which moves in tandem with management rather than automatically against it. And of course that sounds very attractive.

Yes, Germany is a more equal society, I say to Georgia, but in order to be that way it's also a more traditional and less diverse society. Swings and roundabouts. Did you know they have a special word for mothers who work over there? *Rabenmütter,* or raven-mothers. *That's* how conservative they are! And so we go to and fro. We're making history as we go along of course and that's the truth of it; we live in time.

"So what's that wire for?" I asked the man as he took another piece of kit out of his toolbox.

"I push it through drain tube," he said, feeding it into a small hole in the wall joining fridge to freezer. "See. Maybe blockage. Small pieces of food."

"Like my knee!" I said, and told him about the key-hole business.

"Many footballers have this operation," he said, frowning into the fridge. "Cartilage problem."

My brothers stayed put in Middlesbrough and they don't speak to me these days. Earning more than them has done nothing for family relations. All part of the increasingly bitter civil war that's been pitting families against each other up and down the country for some time now: north against south, brother against sister, London against the rest. I moved to London at the right time, I was lucky. This year I've got twenty-eight people on my books.

The man had been here for the best part of an hour now and I started to get a sinking feeling that this was all a waste of time, he'd say he needed to order a spare part or that we'd be better off buying a new fridge-freezer despite the fact this one was only three years old. When I voiced my doubt, though, he assured me he would be able to mend it. Great, I thought.

Even so it was taking a while.

I asked him what he thought of the current Russian president.

"Strong man," he said, with a nod of approval, adjusting a dial behind the vodka bottle.

Strong man? I thought. What, *another* one?

Hadn't they had enough?

A blast from the past: "*What* did you say? *What* did you say?" Beat. Then—"You asked for it!"

Which was what happened if you challenged anything; and, after a while, if you said anything at all. I got up. I got out. I got away. The classic thing is to go for another bully in the future. You don't have to, though.

"Russia needs strong man," he said, going over to the sink to wash his hands.

I looked at his broad shoulders and the way his body tapered at the hips, the elegant triangle of his torso, and this brought to mind the contrasting hunched-back view of the cabdriver who'd driven me home from hospital the night before. He'd wanted to tell me about *his* children; *he'd* had a tale of machismo to tell all right.

He had a grown-up daughter who'd become a hedge fund manager, he said, and she had just come out of a bad relationship.

"Yeah, he was in insurance, the boyfriend. He was all

right the first year, then he got jealous, obsessive jealous if you know what I mean. He started raising his hand to her."

"Nasty," I said.

"My son went round, they had words, then my son he raised his hand to *him* and gave him a bloody good hiding. Lucky it wasn't me, I'd have sent him through the window."

"Yes," I said.

"My son, he got beaten up in Wood Green fifteen years ago. Yeah, Wood Green, funny that"—this said with deep sarcasm—"then after that, after getting beaten up, he went to the gym, he trained in something with a funny name. Like karate but not karate. Anyway, now he can look after himself. And him and his sister, they've always been close."

Sometimes it's hard to know what to say. The last time I heard that expression was when the man I was sitting next to at the Dynamo gala dinner told me, "I have never raised my hand to my wife. To be honest, I've never felt the need to." I think he was expecting me to congratulate him. Well done, sir!

The truth is. The truth is, no one would believe you back then. "A bit heavy-handed" was how it was described if you had to visit A&E. Nothing happened when you told a teacher. The police had a good laugh. "Making a fuss about nothing" was what they used to say; or, if it showed, "making a fuss."

He was still tinkering with the freezer controls. I started to tidy the kitchen, put some mugs in the dishwasher, straightened the pile of books and papers on the dresser.

"My daughter's doing Russian coursework now at school," I told him. "Would you be interested to see her textbook?"

I held it out to show him. He had turned from the freezer to sip his water. He glanced over his shoulder and shook his head.

"But it's about Russia," I said, puzzled.

"Lies," he said.

I blinked. I gave a little laugh before I realised he wasn't joking.

"No, honestly," I said. "It's history."

"Lies," he repeated, compressing his lips, shoving his head back inside the fridge.

Wow, I thought. Bloody hell.

Wait till I tell Nigel he's been barking up the wrong tree all these years, I thought; that he's been wasting his time on Mesopotamia et cetera. Lies! I put the book back in the pile of Verity's coursework on the dresser.

On the evening of my overnight business trip to Moscow Mr. Petrossian had booked a table at a giant marble-clad sushi restaurant. I'd arrived early and was shown to a balcony table from where I could take in the sheer girth of the chandeliers shining light on the men at dinner all around me. The table nearest was occupied by two heavies growling stuff at each other when they weren't growling into their mobiles; opposite them, ignored by them, sat two girls in thick make-up, very young, immobile as captive princesses and completely silent.

I never lied about it but I did stay silent. Secrets aren't the same as lies. It's not something I'm proud of. I told the girls someone got me in the face during a doubles match when they asked about my wavy nose. So it's not true I never lied; I have lied!

Of course, it was another time, the seventies. An earlier stratum of history altogether. And he was plausible, my dad.

I'd had enough. My knee had started to throb and I realised I ought to rest it.

"I have fixed it," said the man triumphantly, closing the freezer door.

He glanced at his watch and scribbled something on his timesheet. I watched him as he started to pack his tools away.

"Well done," I said.

I felt weirdly wiped out.

I knew I ought to ask him what it was that had gone wrong in the first place. I hadn't forgotten about Nigel's file of domestic notes; for some reason though I'd temporarily lost confidence in it. It can't be that useful, I thought, otherwise we'd have got everything sorted ages ago. What if it's not the condenser coils or the evaporator fan next time round? What if it's a different part of the freezer altogether? And even if, thanks to the notes, we do find out what's gone wrong, that won't alter the fact that it's gone wrong again.

I did still ask him though, and I carefully wrote down what he said and dated it. After all, Nigel hadn't once let me down in all the time I'd known him and I had no reason to doubt his way of going about things now. I certainly wasn't going to be the one to foul up his scrupulously recorded dossier.

CHEAPSIDE

"The question is, is it negligence to place a live body in a coffin?" I said, peering at him over my reading glasses.

My job as I understood it was to persuade him that the law can be fun, a good degree course to choose, and to that end I'd dug out an odd little case from a distant back number of the *Law Gazette* to pique his interest.

He was old-fashioned-looking, this boy Sam, thin and fair, with a spotty face and doleful blue eyes. He looked uncomfortable in his shiny sixth-form suit and wore a sullen hunted expression. I wasn't too hopeful of success but I'd promised his father so I ploughed on.

"This case all started with a hitchhiker walking through a Yugoslavian forest in the rain," I said.

"Yugoslavia," he said. "Is that, like, Serbia?"

"That general neck of the woods, yes," I said. "Croatia as well now, and, er, a few others. This was back in the seventies though when it was still all one big communist state."

"I went to Belgrade in the summer," he said, brightening up. "Interrailing."

"Right," I said, quellingly.

Sam's father had sorted me out earlier in the summer after that bout at the gym. He'd overridden me, which isn't easy as anyone will tell you; he'd insisted I go to A&E instead of the meeting I was set on attending, and in so doing he'd probably saved me from something much nastier than a spot of medical balloon magic. Death, even. So when he got on to me about his boy I could hardly refuse. August is a slack month anyway, with the courts in summer recess. These days heart surgery isn't the big deal it used to be; it's more like high-class plumbing crossed with conjuring tricks. They blow up tiny balloons in your arteries to unblock them. No need to open you up! I was back at the office the same week. All pretty seamless.

Anyway, Sam had to decide in the coming school term which subject to take at university. Both his parents were GPs but he was refusing to follow their path so I had been deputed to persuade him that a law degree was a good idea. I was also supposed to offer him some last-minute half-term work experience to include in the all-important personal statement, but from the evidence before my eyes I wasn't sure he was up to more than a spot of light photocopying.

"Your dad was telling me you're not sure yet what subject you want to take at university," I said.

"S'right."

"But you don't want to follow him into medicine."

"Blood," he said, and shuddered.

"What's your favourite A-level subject?"

"Dunno really," he shrugged. "History's OK. Some-times."

"Ah yes, history. That can be a very good route into a legal career, the practice it gives you in analysing events, marshalling information and coming to a conclusion based on the facts."

"I don't *know* what job I want to do," he said with sudden force. "I don't want to decide yet."

"Right."

"Freedom!" he said, giving me a wild look.

"Freedom. Ah yes, freedom versus security. Yes."

"I might take a gap year."

"Erm, I'd think carefully about that if I were you," I said. "We're finding the best universities for law now prefer students not to do that because they 'go off' in the interim, as they put it."

This made him drop his eyes and the corners of his mouth.

"Getting back to our hitchhiker," I said. "After a while, out in the rain, he managed to thumb a lift. The driver nodded at him from his cabin to hop in the back of the open truck. Once on board he wasn't too thrilled to discover a coffin there, but the rain was torrential and he was miles from the next town so he made the best of things and settled down beside it. OK so far?"

"Yeah."

This boy had no responsibilities. He was still a child. Abi is one now and Ava is three. It's a privilege to be doing it all over again and hopefully I'll be able to avoid some of the mistakes I made first time round with Hannah and Martha.

Being wanted by someone, being desired again, and by an attractive young woman like Lauren, that was the most amazing feeling after those years in the post-divorce wilderness. Less so since the babies of course, but still! Yes, OK, Lauren is young enough to be my daughter, as Hannah and Martha have pointed out more than once. But that only makes me realise how lucky I am to get a second chance. It also makes me see I have a responsibility to look after my health and ensure I live another good few years if I want to see Abi and Ava through university. No more steak frites for me!

"He'd been sitting there for a little while, our hitchhiker," I continued, "when the lid of the coffin lifted and a voice asked, 'Has the rain stopped?' This caused him to scream out in terror and then to leap from the moving truck, breaking his leg in the process."

"Idiot."

"Why?"

" 'Cos he overreacted," said Sam.

"Are you ready to order, sir?" said the waiter, appearing with his notepad.

"Another couple of minutes, please," I said, turning my attention back to the menu.

No oysters, of course; no R in "August." Fried whitebait, smoked eel, skate with black butter. I'd chosen this hundred-year-old fish restaurant partly to give Sam a dose of City tradition, but mainly because I'm trying to be sensible since the stents. I chose skate, on the grounds that it's more substantial than other fish. Without the black butter, obviously.

He was seventeen, this boy, and I was fifty-six. What he didn't know was that keeping his options open now would likely lead to extra hard work later on. I wasn't at all sure about his parents' enthusiasm for law anyway. Every bright kid these days is doing a law degree or a law conversion course and it's massively oversubscribed as a profession. Be that as it may, this wasn't the message his parents wanted to hear so I soldiered on.

"You could do history at university then take a law conversion course afterwards," I said. "That would defer things a bit."

That's what they're doing now after degrees in anthropology or history or Old Icelandic, the children of my colleagues—a law conversion course. At vast expense to their parents I might add. My own girl Hannah has insisted on taking this route, so I should know. Funny, the four of us together again at her graduation in June. Bev had gone grey since the last time I saw her. She hadn't had it cut, her wild woman hair, and it looked quite eccentric. Lauren's is smooth as glass.

"Of course, if the law conversion course is not an option you could try entering a law firm at a lower level," I told Sam. "Go in as a paralegal."

"What, like a paramedic?" he said, looking alarmed.

"Not exactly," I said. "No."

I worked out early on that I'd have to be a lawyer. I couldn't do science and I didn't want to teach: ergo, the law. And getting paid to argue for a living sounded all right to me. Bev used to say that in the unlikely event of my being assigned a coat of arms, one of its quarters would have to feature the hind leg of a donkey.

At the time I did my articles female lawyers were still pretty thin on the ground, though by the time we divorced they were all over the place. Naturally enough women will often go part-time once they have children, but they're still very well rewarded in this profession and provide a high-quality second-tier service. Because you can't be in charge of a big case and not give it everything, that's the thing, and that's what Bev never was able to understand. The work comes in intense bursts, sometimes for several weeks at a time, and obviously your personal life is going to have to go on hold to a certain extent when that happens.

She was too emotional.

"What's a Buck Rarebit?" asked the boy.

"It's a Welsh Rarebit with a poached egg on top."

"What's a Welsh Rarebit?"

"It's cheese on toast," I said. "Don't they teach you anything at school?"

His face turned red, deeper and deeper as I watched, even his forehead.

"Only joking," I said, thinking to myself that he wasn't going to get very far without a bit more bounce.

We met at the height of punk at some student party in Corpus where everyone was pogoing beneath the medieval rafters, jump-dancing competitively—ridiculous!—and Bev, who was reading history, was laughing at me and the other law students as we all danced to "I Fought the Law and the Law Won." Whatever happened to punk, eh? I've still got my vinyl forty-fives in lime green and bubble-gum pink—the Sex Pistols, Siouxsie and the Banshees, the Clash.

I looked around the room for the waiter so we could order. The shiny cream paint, the wood panelling and the steel jugs of tartare sauce gave it a collegiate feel, as did the watercolour cartoons of nineteenth-century statesmen up at cornice level and the framed signed cricket bats and sports shirts in glass boxes on the walls.

We were both part of that brief wave when Oxbridge let the oiks in. My father managed a branch of Mac Fisheries in Southport and hers was a school caretaker in Lewisham, the old bugger. That was in the late seventies with the whole country in the doldrums and us separately doing our homework by candlelight during the three-day week. There was much doom and gloom at that point about the end of days, but then we surfed into the eighties and everything went global.

Our generation was lucky. The whole world opened up. All sorts of not terribly bright people have done extremely well in the last thirty years. They've had to put in the hours, sure; but even the ones who didn't work hard and had no ambition have done all right compared with their parents. If they lived down south, that is. And lots of us did up sticks and move down south during that time.

Bev used to say, Why not employ double the lawyers and pay them half? It would still be plenty and that way they'd get some life outside work too. She just didn't get it. There *is* no such thing as the work-life balance. That's the point! You cannot be both driven *and* laid-back. You either step up to the plate and embrace the fourteen-hour day, or you don't. Sure, there's life outside work if you're a lawyer. But that doesn't mean never working through the night or a holiday—sorry!

"You know the story of the ant and the grasshopper, Sam?" I asked.

"Yeah," he said, morose. "My dad already told me it."

"Right," I said. "So. Back to our hitchhiker and his broken leg."

"The idiot."

I was beginning to think I should have fallen back on the usual hackneyed example, the one about whether it's ever OK to eat a cabin boy.

It's a question of attitude, I wanted to tell him; it's to do with stamina and combative strength; courage, even. I mean, for example, the rugby player who reset his dislocated knee on the pitch and carried on.

"What's your favourite sport?" I asked him.

"I don't like sport."

That figured.

It was fine for our parents: job security and next to no unemployment. You worked not very hard and you had enough. A job with a proper pension, too! Those were the days. But it's been different for us and this was what I wanted to get over to Sam before we finished the meal. Now there is no halfway house, not even in the public sector.

Bev said, Enough's enough: we're lucky and we've grown up in a country with free schools and health care so let's move outside London and make the most of it. She suggested I move away from the City, practise in the country, a bit of light probate and conveyancing, but what she didn't understand was, they're really struggling now, those two-horse outfits. Everyone accepts that we'll never see a return to the stability that was once a hallmark of our profession.

Also I would have found that boring.

"After a certain point the more a man earns the less I think of him," Bev said. Ridiculous. "Oh, and what point would that be?" I asked her. "The point of elegant sufficiency," she said. Which was like a private joke we had; it was what her grandmother in Catford used to say when she asked us whether we'd had enough to eat: Have you had sufficient? We used to go there for Sunday lunch or tea, all those years before we had children.

Lauren has nothing of the old hippie about her, I'm glad to say. No, Lauren has her head screwed on all right.

Bev decided to take the shame of world economic

inequality on her own shoulders, the guilt at global greed. As if it hasn't always been like this! Any normal woman would have been proud of what we'd achieved. It's not like we inherited anything—we never had a bean from our families. Whereas Lauren has a healthy sense of entitlement. Maybe it's a generational thing.

Divorce is no fun. No. I'm surprised how it still rankles, this much further down the line. But, life goes on.

The waiter arrived with a big pale meaty wing of skate for me and a small scorched slice of toasted cheese for the boy.

"Are you sure that's all you want?" I asked. "Are you slimming or something?"

Again he blushed that furious shade of crimson.

"I don't like fish," he mumbled, glancing at the pile on my plate and recoiling.

"Ah, that is unfortunate," I said.

I should have taken him for a sandwich in the crypt of St. Mary-le-Bow and had done with it. Then I could have pointed out the churches dovetailed between City highrises, the way a Wren church will cradle an office block in the crook of its arm. I could have shown him the figure of Justice on top of the Old Bailey with a sword in her right hand and the scales of justice in her left, and that would probably have had more of an effect on him than this lunch seemed to be doing.

"So," I said. "Let's return to our hitchhikers."

He looked at me hopelessly.

"What had happened, of course, was that an earlier

hitchhiker, let's call him Hitchhiker One, had got into the back of the truck and decided to climb inside the empty coffin, pulling the lid over himself to keep the rain off. He heard the truck stop for another hitchhiker, our man, whom we will call Hitchhiker Two, but he didn't come out of the coffin at that point because he could still hear the rain pouring down. Then, after a while, when the rain sounded less heavy, he lifted the lid and we know what happened next."

"Yeah, he broke his leg."

"So what do you think?"

"Hitchhiker Two was an idiot," said Sam. "And Hitchhiker One was a nutter. To get into a coffin."

"Why? He would say just common sense. If you haven't got the sense to come in out of the rain . . ."

"He should have waited for a covered truck, shouldn't he, if he didn't want to get wet."

"Well, he didn't," I snapped.

Us lot, the lawyers from my sort of background, the ones who watched *Crown Court* on television after school, we thought we'd be criminal lawyers. Ha. Now this lot are saying they only want to do human rights cases. Double ha. Ha ha! Of course we got siphoned off into corporate tax, or commercial property, or dispute resolution.

Bev said lawyers are the little birds that fly into the open mouth of the crocodile so as to feed on the scraps of decaying meat between its teeth; pretty low down the food chain, she used to scoff. Luckily I'm fairly thick-skinned. You have to be, if you're a lawyer. Let's kill all the lawyers! That's Shakespeare. We're probably on a par with politicians in the popularity stakes, which figures: every other politician these days will be or will have been a lawyer.

"Sam," I said, "I think we need to take a more granular and nuanced approach."

I was starting to lose patience.

"The way that English law would approach this," I continued, "is by looking at whether the tort of negligence has been committed. You know what tort is?"

"No."

"It's a wrongful act in cases where there is no contract, leading to civil legal liability."

He looked clueless, puzzled and depressed.

"You know what a contract is?"

"Like when you make a deal?"

"Correct," I said, a touch wearily. "A contract is a written or spoken agreement enforceable by law and I think we can both see that our hitchhiker and truck driver hadn't made a contract. Clear so far?"

He nodded.

"Here, negligence is a tort because there was nothing agreed in speech or writing; there was no mutual bargain or exchange on the cards. OK?"

He nodded again, without enthusiasm.

"And the question an English court would ask would probably be, was there sufficient proximity in this case for either the truck driver or Hitchhiker One to assume a duty of care to Hitchhiker Two?"

He stared down at his plate and started to tear little pellets off his bread roll.

"Do you follow me?" I asked.

"Sort of," he mumbled.

Sort of, I thought; not good enough.

"All right, I'll try to be clearer," I said. "'Proximity' is the legal word for a relationship that's close enough to give rise to a duty of care."

"What's a duty of care?"

"What do you think it is?"

"It sounds like something you have to do if you get married."

"Eh?"

"Or have children. You ought to care for them. It's your duty to care for them."

"No," I said. "That's not it."

I sighed.

"Look, I'll give you an example," I went on. "If I offer someone a lift in my car that means I've got a duty of care towards them. OK so far?"

He nodded.

"It's my duty to make sure the car is roadworthy and that my driving is safe. I've got a duty of care to my passenger. Yes?"

"OK."

"So do you think the truck driver has a duty of care towards any hitchhikers he might pick up?"

"Not if he doesn't ask them into his truck; not if they ask themselves."

"Ah, so you would argue, would you, that if you ask yourself along for the ride, anything that happens after that is at your own risk?"

"Yeah."

"Then you would be pleading the doctrine *Volenti non fit injuria!*"

"Eh?"

He goggled at me, startled, blue eyes flying wide open.

"To a willing person no injury is done."

"Yeah," he said. "No."

Things reached breaking point when we got to forty-three. Classic midlife crisis stuff I suppose. Two children, a great big mortgage and she was still refusing to take my career seriously. "It's not war time!" she said. "There's no *need* to live like this." She called me the absentee landlord. She said I only stopped off at home to refuel; that I'd turned the house into a garage. I wanted to hang on to her and the children and not be there at the same time, she said; that was me having my cake and eating it according to her. When I look back it was like having a fifth columnist in the house, constantly criticising and undermining.

She didn't exactly have any helpful suggestions as to what I should do about it. Retrain as a teacher? A cab driver? I think not. In the heat of the moment I referred to her little job in arts admin as a "luxury" and of course she remembered that. "I earn my keep! I pay my way!"

But it *was* a luxury by that point. Considering how little she earned it would have been much easier all round if she'd just accepted that the domestic side of things and the childcare was all down to her and simply got on with it; stopped all that farcical talk of juggling and sharing, all the bloody moaning. Compared with what I'd started to bring in, the money she earned was pathetic. But she refused to stop working; she said that would be like taking the King's shilling and if she did that she'd forfeit her right to speak out.

Lauren's current part-time job in HR brings in significantly more than Bev's ever did, but *she* doesn't bang on about it all the time. She knows whose job is more important. It's the job of the one who earns the most. Obviously.

I had been scraping pale ribbons of flesh from the skate's ribbed wing all this while. It hadn't seemed terribly fresh, the fish, but I was hungry and had tucked in. Eventually, though, I could ignore the ammoniac whiff no longer. It smelt of urine and I should know, with two infants at home still in nappies. I called the waiter over.

"It's fresh, sir," he said. "I saw it come in myself this morning."

He took my proffered plate and sniffed the remaining fish.

"It won't *harm* you," he added.

There was a pause.

"Do you want to say something about it to the manager?" he asked halfheartedly.

I glanced at Sam, who was looking decidedly green around the gills at this little conversation, and decided against. No, enough fish, I said; but some more bread rolls, please. And the pudding menu.

We were deep into the dog days of summer, after all, and nowhere near the sea.

Matters came to a head when I got the offer of partnership from a Magic Circle firm. Any normal woman would have been thrilled for me but she said if it meant me working more hours then I shouldn't take it. She said that would be unreasonable. Unreasonable! *She* was the unreasonable one.

Be home two nights a week by eight so we can eat together, she said; if I promised to be back two nights a week by eight then she'd back me up and carry on. *She* was the unreasonable one! There was no way I could promise that if I joined the Magic Circle, there was just no way. Not two nights; not *one* night.

"Have you heard of the Magic Circle?" I asked Sam now as he pored over the puddings on the menu.

"Yes!" he said, to my surprise, perking up.

"What do you know about it?" I asked.

"It's the premier organisation in the world."

"Well, you're on the right track," I said, sitting back, rather pleased at this development. Maybe he wasn't as clueless as he looked after all. "Did your parents tell you about it? Or the school careers people, maybe?"

"No," he said, looking puzzled. "I went to an open day with my friends."

"An open day?"

"Yeah. It was brilliant. We're going to join when we're eighteen."

"I'm not sure it works like that," I said, light slowly dawning. "What open day *was* this?"

"They have regular open days at their headquarters in Euston," he said.

"Who do?"

"The Magic Circle."

"Hang on a minute," I said. "What happened at this open day?"

"They did these really unbelievable card tricks," he told me earnestly. "But even the ones with coins were amazing."

I sighed.

He started some feat of legerdemain involving his grubby shirt cuff and a 50p coin.

"Never mind," I said. "Never mind."

Anyway, I joined the Magic Circle and my wife jumped ship. I didn't think she'd do it but she did. The lady vanished. I ignored her objections and accepted the offer assuming, of course, that she'd see sense. "Money is enough for some people I suppose," was what she said. "But for anyone with a heart this way of life is brutal." I assumed she'd eventually come round; that she'd stop all the sobbing and going on at me in the middle of the night. I simply couldn't afford to pay too much attention to that sort of carry-on at the time. Next thing I knew she'd gone, taking the children with her. "What's the point," she said. "You're never there."

Divorce is the most expensive thing you'll ever do, I wanted to tell the boy; might as well give him some useful advice to take away from the lunch. Sometimes I feel a spurt of anger that Bev didn't chuck in her little job and spend her energies on buy-to-let like other cannier women I could mention. Lauren's mother, for instance. Then I might have been able to ease up a bit more at this stage. As it is, the golf course is nothing but a distant mirage in the desert.

She's running some festival now in Norwich with a man with a ponytail. Poetry, yoga, that sort of thing. She was always on about balance and now she can stand on one leg for five minutes with her eyes shut. Good for her. She organises courses in mindfulness too. Breathe in, breathe out. Amazing what you can charge for these days.

Part of why I haven't progressed quite as planned at work was that I did go slightly overboard at one point, on the self-medication front as I think it's now called. Luckily I stopped in time, with Lauren's help. Lauren was in our HR department, she saw what was happening and she saved me. She really was my human resource! She showed me love when I was at a very low ebb and for that I owe her an enormous debt of gratitude.

"What's Spotted Dick?" asked Sam, looking up from the menu with the suggestion of a smirk.

"It's a currant and suet pudding which they serve in

slices with custard," I said reprovingly. Not nearly as disgusting as it sounds, actually, but there was no way Spotted Dick was on the menu for me anymore. Strawberries, hold the cream; that would have to do me.

I'd been feeling below par at the gym when it happened. I'd told myself not to be such a wuss and made myself increase the incline on the running machine. Just before I fell off and blacked out the thought flashed into my mind, Oh Christ, are my chargeable hours up to date? And amazingly, as I fell, I remembered that they were.

Lauren sees an action-packed future for us, the four of us off on adventure-discovery holidays as soon as the girls are old enough. Zip wires across the Amazon rain forest, gorillas in volcanic craters, that sort of thing. The Galápagos Islands have been mentioned. I can't help wondering whether she's anticipating my demise and planning lots of visual evidence for the photo album in advance. Very proactive, Lauren.

Somebody's got to be responsible. Somebody's got to take care of that side of things. Diet and exercise! Think of your heart as a piece of chewing gum said the physio; if you don't stretch it and chew it all the time it hardens into an inelastic lump.

"So was it reasonably foreseeable that an injury could arise?" I continued, making an effort. "What do you think, Sam?"

Tenacity is the name of the game; he'd better get used to that fact if he was going to be a lawyer.

"Not really, as regards the truck driver, was it," I persisted. "The truck driver stayed in the dry in his front seat so no, he couldn't reasonably foresee that a hitchhiker would lie in the coffin. Do you agree?"

"Yeah," said Sam.

Most lawyers these days marry other people in the same sort of job so both parties know what they're signing up for. Bev didn't sign up for that, she didn't know the deal, and I suppose that was my mistake—trying to make her live a life she hadn't signed up for.

"Come on, Sam, was it reasonably foreseeable that an injury could arise as regards the actions of Hitchhiker One?" I chivvied him. "This could be argued with more chance of success. To rise up out of a coffin asking if the rain's gone off—yes, in most people's minds they might feel embarrassed or worried about causing alarm by so doing."

"Yeah," said the boy unexpectedly. "Hitchhiker One was wrong if anyone. He didn't, like, *think*. He didn't put himself in the other one's place."

"Ah, failure of imagination. Not actually a legal offence," I said. "Though some might argue it ought to be."

"He was just thinking of himself."

"That's not a crime."

"But he was *stupid*!"

"Still not a crime."

I'm very much at the stage now of *not* scaling back. With Hannah going in for a law conversion course and Martha wanting to take a masters in psychology I'll be shelling out for them both for a while yet. Not to mention the hefty deposits they'll need when they come to buy. As for Abi and Ava, Lauren quite rightly wants our daughters to have the same advantages as their sisters, so it looks like I'll be staying very much in harness for the foreseeable future.

Things don't necessarily get easier at work as you progress in seniority. It's recently been made clear that it won't be viable for me to maintain my place on the lockstep. Unless. That word! Unless I put in the next few years sorting out the Dubai office. There's also talk of switching our remuneration system from lockstep to merit-based— or Eat-What-You-Kill as it's more commonly known. Which would not be good news for me at this stage. So I'd better nail down the proposed arrangement pronto.

It did make me think twice, I'll admit it. The time I'd gone to our Dubai office to consult our man Russell McKie, I got the distinct impression he'd gone slightly mad. Out there for the school fees: grew up on a housing scheme himself but his sons are down for Eton. Talk-talk-talk, he wouldn't let me get a word in edgeways. He was too much on his own with his thoughts, that was the impression I got.

It's a really enormous airport, Dubai, and it was absolutely heaving with people when I arrived at three in the morning. Then there were miles of gigantic motorways and flyovers. The pillars of the flyover supports were incredibly fancy and decorated. Everything was new. It was all unreal somehow. I didn't really take to it.

But needs must and I'm no spring chicken. Highly

responsive legal solutions in every time zone, we're passionate about that, and Dubai is obviously key to this strategy, sitting on the time line as it does. It's the place the Middle East has decided it'll do business with the West.

Skype helps, apparently. You can be there on-screen for the bedtime story, Russell was telling me, so that's something. Lauren wants to stay in Putney so she can be near her mother and also keep her job ticking over. They'll come out for holidays, though not between May and October of course when it's forty-five, fifty in the shade and the sea gets too hot for swimming.

I'm boning up on sharia law at the weekends, Murabaha and all its crafty ways of getting round direct involvement with usury. Now *that* really is having your cake and eating it!

And of course I won't need to pay tax, so two years there will be the same as four years back home. Maybe. If they keep me at the same level on the lockstep.

One part of me wishes she'd come out with the babies to live with me in Dubai; but I don't think anything I say would persuade her. She's extremely determined, Lauren, when she's made her mind up.

I'll be able to get some reading done in my spare time, as she pointed out the other day, some of those mega novels I've not had time for till now. *War and Peace; Moby-Dick!*

I should be back in plenty of time to plan a blowout sixtieth birthday party if my heart behaves itself.

"So, where are we after all that?" I said, polishing off the last of my strawberries. "What's your verdict, Sam? Eh?"

"Guilty," said Sam, scraping the remains of his jam roll from the plate.

"The word 'guilty' is normally associated with criminal law," I said. "But we'll let that pass. I think we've established a clear case of negligence on the part of Hitchhiker One, though, don't you?"

"Definitely."

He met my eye and broke into a grin, probably in relief that it was almost over.

"Thanks for lunch," he added.

"A pleasure," I said, trying to attract the waiter's attention for the bill.

This boy wasn't the only one who was eager to be off. I had a two-thirty meeting at Crutched Friars with a visiting lawyer from the Bulgarian Water Company we were dealing with, and I'd have to get a move on now if I was going to be on time.

"So then," I said once we were outside on the pavement, shaking his hand, "good luck with everything."

"Same to you!" he said with another guileless smile. He had jam on his tie, I noticed.

As I scanned the horizon for a cab I watched him walk away from me into the sunny afternoon and I wondered why his hands were up underneath his chin. Next thing I saw, he was tearing his tie off and stuffing it into his pocket. I didn't envy his parents. He wriggled his shoulders, gave a little skip like a goat or a lamb, then started to run. I don't know where he thought he was going; he was heading in completely the wrong direction for where he'd come from. I was surprised how fast he was, though; he was really flying down Cheapside. I wouldn't have thought he had it in him. Then my BlackBerry buzzed and when I looked up again he must have disappeared off down Bread Street.

ARIZONA

18:07 | NEEDLES

"Can you feel that?"

"Ouch. Yes."

"Good."

"A sort of pulling sensation. Is that right?"

" 'The therapeutic ache.' Yes."

She felt like a violin being tuned, she thought, as she stared up at the ceiling. The twisting of the hair-fine needles along with the checking of various pulse points made it feel like some sort of fine-tuning was going on.

"And that?" asked Mae again, turning another needle.

"Yes, but not as strongly," Liz replied.

It seemed to work by administering little shocks to get things moving again. Stalled fluids. All the chronic stuff doctors hated, that's what it was supposed to be good for; autoimmune conditions, IBS, asthma, backache. From what she'd understood.

"Was the migraine less severe this time, would you say?" asked Mae. "In terms of intensity?"

"No," said Liz. "Unfortunately not. Worse if anything.

Flashing lights, nausea; flat on my back in a darkened room. But it may all simply disappear when I hit the menopause! You said so last time."

"That does happen sometimes," said Mae, raising her eyebrows slightly and smiling. "I'm not offering empty hope."

They lapsed back into silence while Mae stood and held Liz's wrist, testing her pulse. Quite a lot of any acupuncture session seemed to be filled with this careful pulse-taking. As far as she had understood, there were twelve different pulse points, six along each wrist, all useful for reading the selfsame central pulse in subtly different diagnostic ways. And the changes in pulse quality that happened when Mae slid a new needle into one of the body's eight hundred or so acupuncture points provided her with clues as to what should be done next. Or something like that. At any rate it was a quiet, painstaking business as well as a leap of faith, and Liz was finding it surprisingly restful.

The room was bare and clean and bright, though without the strip-lit glare of the hospital space where she had last week seen the specialist. "Be happy," he had said, patronisingly, at the end of an inconclusive appointment. Her GP had snorted when she told her this: "Another consultant telling a middle-aged woman she's hysterical." Certainly his advice had not been noticeably more scientific than anything Mae had said so far.

"So, what are you working on now?" asked Mae, returning her arm carefully to the table.

"I'm finishing a paper on the Risorgimento for a con-
ference at Senate House next week. Mazzini's identifica-
tion of liberty with blood sacrifice, all that."

"The Risorgimento?"

"It was the big freedom movement of the nineteenth
century."

"Yes, yes," murmured Mae mock-seriously, then: "I
don't know what you're talking about but it all sounds
very impressive."

Mae had been recommended to Liz by an insomniac
colleague in the history faculty. He had earnestly assured
her that he felt better than he had done for months and
that a needle between the brows was the sovereign rem-
edy against sleeplessness; Liz had decided to go along
with an open mind.

"He *was* quite impressive, Mazzini. In exile all those
years. He never gave up. Though Marx did call him 'that
everlasting old ass.'"

"History passed me by," shrugged Mae. "I couldn't take
the rules at school, the lack of freedom. I did no work. I
was a rebel."

"I was a swot," said Liz. "I've never really stopped being one."

"Um," said Mae. "I was quite wild."

"It doesn't seem to have done you any harm!"

"I don't know about that."

They lapsed back into silence. How strange and welcome, thought Liz, the distant intimacy which had sprung
up between them. They could afford to say anything that

came into their heads since they had zero contact with each other outside this bare quiet room. Lying on Mae's padded table seemed to liberate all sorts of illuminated ramblings, which, combined with the sporadic nature of the treatment, made for an unusually dreamy, intermittent sort of conversation.

18:15 | GOTHIC

While she had been taking Liz's health history in the preliminary session, Mae had laughed and commented that the two of them happened to be almost exactly the same age. Born in the same month fifty years ago, both were coalescing a step deeper into middle age. What would it be like, now wondered Liz, this shift away from the heightened sensitivity which regularly, tidally, made itself felt in advance of blood? And, parrying her own embarrassed, automatic self-accusation of self-indulgence: why *shouldn't* the private life of the body be acknowledged as it crossed this new threshold?

"Aren't we supposed to feel fear and loathing about it?" she said now.

"I don't," said Mae. "Do you?"

"No," said Liz, with slight surprise. "But other people seem to. Younger women. Men. I haven't mentioned it to anyone else except you, because of that."

"It does creep men out," admitted Mae. "The very mention of it. But then, so does any mention of periods."

"Even the language is Gothic, isn't it—the Curse and the Change."

"The Change!" said Mae. "Very doomy, yes. But menopause isn't much better. It even *sounds* miserable and moany."

"Moanapause."

They both started to laugh, quietly.

Sometimes when she woke from a flabbergasting dream Liz would lie very still to see if she could net it before it fled; perfectly still, eyes closed, not moving her head, as if the slightest shift would tip the story-bearing liquid, break its fragile meniscus and spill the night's elusive catch. Here she had to be still too, even rocking gently with laughter as she was now, in order not to displace the various long fine silvery needles which bristled from her face and arms and fingers and toes, and which quivered slightly as she moved.

"Also, had you noticed?" she said, once their laughter had died away. "Calling a woman menopausal is the ultimate insult."

"I thought that was the C-word," said Mae, eyes downcast, professionally circumspect. "The ultimate insult."

"Except that's a noun, and 'menopausal' is an adjective. 'Menopausal' is used to write you off, isn't it."

"Yes."

"Whereas the C-word carries more hatred."

"It's what men call other men," commented Mae.

"Is it? Yes, you're right—I suppose it is."

"In Russia they call it your money-maker," said Mae. "The C-word."

"How nasty! No, we're not having that."

Les Grandes Horizontales, she thought, gazing up at the ceiling; wasn't that what they used to call the courtesans of nineteenth-century Paris? At least we're now allowed paid employment in other areas; equal pay, sometimes. But yes, upwardly mobile; vertical job opportunities. In much of the world, anyway.

"In Chinese traditional medicine they call it the Gate of Mystery," added Mae, after a long pause. "Also, the coital muscle."

"Hmm. Interesting. But neither of those will do either really."

"No."

"There's always 'vagina' of course, but I've never liked that because I did Latin at school, Caesar's *Gallic Wars,* and it's Latin for scabbard. Still, I suppose it's the best of a bad bunch."

There was a pause.

"I'm certainly not calling it a coochie or a foo-foo or whatever the latest suggestion is," she added.

"No," said Mae. "I find I don't want to personalise it in that way."

"You're right. Neither do I. And that's how it should be. That's OK. If there was a good name they'd only take it and trash it."

18:19 | AUGUST

It can be useful for chronic conditions that flare up, Mae had told her, mildly, at the start of these sessions. If it brings inflammation down and holds it down, acupunc-

ture can give more years not dominated by the condi-
tion; inflammation that flares up and feeds on itself is not
great. As for the menopause she, Mae, had observed from
her clients that it seemed to be pure luck of the draw how
it affected you.

"Some women are unlucky and have a bad time,"
came her voice from behind Liz as she stood at the head
of the table and checked the needles in her scalp. "Night
sweats. Drenched sheets. They have to get up and change
their sheets in the middle of the night."

"Not us!" said Liz, rolling her eyes back in her head at
her like a racehorse.

"Of course not," said Mae drily.

They were quiet. Mae moved to the wooden chair in a
corner of the room and sat checking her notes.

"It's interesting," she said at last. "Your migraines do
tend to occur in the same week of your cycle."

That heavy dream-dogged sleep of the week before,
thought Liz; the headache and slowness and central
unwillingness to stir: would these disappear along with
the heady waterlogged desire to be inward?

"I realise I think of the menopause as extra time," said
Mae. "If I'd been born elsewhere in the world I might
easily have died long before now."

"Yes," said Liz. "Or, a hundred years ago, here, of
course. Pure luck. It would help though if we knew where-
abouts we were on the scale now, wouldn't it. Towards the
end? In the middle?"

"I like to think we're somewhere around August," said Mae dreamily. "The very end of summer."

August, thought Liz: the quick chill in the middle of brightness and warmth; confident wasteful growth starting to go to seed. Something casual and wild about it. Confidence. Strength. The smell of dust, and sudden thunderstorms.

"I'll tell you my own idea of it," continued Mae. "Here and now. For us."

She paused and lifted Liz's arm again, silently counting for a few seconds.

"There's a sort of game I play when I'm trying to get to sleep where I parcel out the years," she continued. "So, up to the age of ten, when you're still in waiting and time goes slowly, that's when you're in January and February. From ten to twenty it's March and April. Then it's May, which takes you all the way to thirty since you're fully in the world at last."

"OK," said Liz, smiling. "And at that rate, June is your thirties, July your forties, August your fifties."

"September until sixty-nine, that's autumn," continued Mae. "Early old age, whatever anybody says. Then October is the seventies, that can still be early to middle-old age if you're lucky; and November and December are middle to proper old age, because let's face it, we're probably not going to make it beyond a hundred."

"August sounds good," said Liz.

18:24 | *SHIBUI*

"Now, if you'll close your eyes I'm going to try something new. I'm going to try some needles in the eye sockets."

"Really? Give me a moment," said Liz. "I could never have a face lift, could I. OK. Go ahead."

She closed her eyes and freewheeled into her thoughts, breathing through the little shock as the needles were inserted one at a time.

"So how do you feel about looking older?" she asked, eyes still closed. "Do you care?"

The room was quiet for a while.

"It's harder in some professions than others," said Mae at last. "I have a client, she's an actress, she's quite famous. You know what they say about an older woman having to choose between her face and her bum? Well, she chose her bum and she tells me she wishes she hadn't."

"Serves her right."

"But still."

"Talking of which," said Liz. "Have you noticed how you never can tell from a man's face how big his bum is going to be?"

Mae cast her gaze up at the ceiling and considered. There was silence.

"That's true," she conceded after a while. "That's very true."

There was a pause while they thought about this, Liz with her eyes shut and Mae gazing out of the window, giggling gently, waves of submerged laughter rippling through them.

"She's also gone down the Botox route, this same client," continued Mae after a while. "She's had little bits of work done and she does look younger than her age. But *she* doesn't think she looks good, so what's the point? She groans when she looks in the mirror."

Yes, the challenge is to see whether you can carry on liking your own face, thought Liz. There is such a thing as the beauty of ageing. The Japanese have a word for it, don't they—*shibui*. I leave anemones in their vase for as long as I can, tulips too, for those wild swoops they do on their way out, the way their stems curve and lunge and shed soot-dusted petals. In fact I like them best at that stage. I'm not a vase of flowers, though, am I.

"Is that all right?" asked Mae, adjusting a needle. "Can you feel that?"

"Ouch. Yes."

But let's not luxuriate in self-disgust, continued Liz, taking herself to task. We wouldn't riff on how hideous our grandmothers look—it's disrespectful of life, that sort of cruelty, for one thing. It's childish to criticise people for looking older. Including ourselves. And the cruelty comes from fear.

"I honestly don't think I've ever loved anyone less for growing older," she said now. "For looking older. Even friends where I've started off drawn to them by their looks. In fact, I usually love them more because they've become more vulnerable. I feel extra tenderness on top of everything else. I love them *more*. Don't you find that?"

"Mmm," said Mae. "Not sure."

Some of the people I've loved most in my life have been quite old, thought Liz. One or two have been *very* old—the ones who've continued to change and grow. And some of them—particularly the ones who've had worldly success—have probably been much nicer and more interesting older than in their unkind powerful youth. They've acquired vulnerability.

"OK, then, say it hasn't made you love them less," said Mae. "Has it made you *fancy* them less, though?"

"Oh," said Liz. "Ah. Yes. Let me have a think."

"Because it's about that, isn't it," said Mae, starting to remove the needles from her eye sockets with practised deftness.

18:31 | SEX

"Yes, it is interesting, all that," said Liz, opening her eyes. "I am interested in what happens about, um, sex. I mean, at what age that's supposed to stop."

Mae raised her eyebrows as she contemplated the fan of needles in her left hand, and looked thoughtful.

"They say," she said cautiously, "they say the menopause takes women one of two ways. Either they grow more libidinous. Or the opposite."

"What, it can just turn off?" said Liz, also raising her eyebrows.

"Maybe it happens that one day you stop wanting to. And then you find you don't regret what you don't want."

"Maybe," said Liz doubtfully.

She, Liz, was still married to the girls' father though there was little opportunity for sex anymore—most nights he was up and waiting for the return of one or the other of them, texting and swearing and generally on their case. There was always the possibility that a daughter would return early from a disappointing night and walk in on them. Their bedroom had become a general family meeting place over the years, incorrigibly domesticated—Christmas stockings; sick children being cosseted; forum for passionate and extensive discussions about vital matters (like when bedtime was); meeting place for postmortems of fascinating teen evenings and resumés of movies watched. He had suggested a bolt on the door; she had worried that would seem unfriendly; he had fixed one, nonetheless. "Ha ha ha, they're trying to have sex," came the voices from the other side. In the service of tact as when under parental roofs of their youth they persisted in grim silence, clenching their teeth.

"I do have clients who say they feel nothing but relief now that 'all that,' as they put it, is over," said Mae, opening a new packet of needles. "I'm going to try your right temple next."

Liz drew a long slow breath and closed her eyes again. Into her mind floated the lunchtime concert she'd attended at St. Pancras Church last week, Schubert's *Death and the Maiden*. Most of the heads in the audience had been white- or grey-haired. And she hadn't been able to help noticing the smell: nothing awful, just the subdued but unmistakable smell of underwashed jumpers and hair that had been left to go an extra day. They weren't expecting anything.

"I can't see how you wouldn't regret the loss of that," she said.

Regret was surely too dilute a word.

"I've heard it's sixty, sixty-five," she continued. "That sixty-five's about average. For women *and* men."

"It can go on to seventy," said Mae. "Eighty."

"Eighty?"

"It would be different, though," said Mae thoughtfully. "Older. Different things."

"Yes?"

"Communication would be key."

"How do you mean?"

But Mae had lapsed into silence again.

18:37 | SANDWICH

Her own girls, fifteen and sixteen, were at the start of it all. They still hadn't got used to their bodies gearing up, thought Liz with a pang; they oscillated between pride and outrage at the new conditions of life to which they now saw they would have to reconcile themselves (and in strict silence, too, publicly at least). Presently emerging into lunar beauty they were virulently critical of her appearance and frighteningly sensitive about their own. They shudder at my arms, Liz thought, at my elbows; but they're savagely self-policing too. It's all part and parcel. I wish I could make them know how effortlessly beautiful they are.

"It's when you come out the other side," said Liz now. "Isn't it."

"The other side of what?"

"All *that*. The reproductive life. If you've had children. Even if you haven't. It's when you're returned to yourself. So they say."

"My middle daughter is in a bulimic phase just now," shrugged Mae. "Meanwhile my mother's lost it; she opens the door with nothing on."

"Wow."

"Yeah."

She twirled the needle in the crook of Liz's right elbow.

"Can you feel that?"

"Ouch. Yes. They call us the sandwich generation, you know," continued Liz. "They're trying to blame us again, of course. Caught between teenagers and aged parents and all because we left having children until our thirties. But it doesn't wash!"

She paused and scowled up at the ceiling.

"I know a woman of sixty-four who had her children in her early twenties," she continued. "And now she's having to deal with her ninety-three-year-old father as well as house one of her divorced daughters and provide hefty chunks of childcare for various baby grandchildren."

"She doesn't have to," said Mae coolly.

"True," admitted Liz, momentarily confounded.

There was a pause.

"Though sometimes it seems boundless, what you give," she added.

"It's not, though," said Mae. "Boundless. Is it."

"Isn't it?"

"Once in a while I leave them all to it, I always have done. Every now and then I need to cut loose. Travel."

"How?" said Liz.

"I call in a few favours," shrugged Mae. "Set up some basic support. Youth hostels have no age limit. I have my life to think of too."

"How do you not feel guilty?" said Liz after a while.

"I do feel guilt but I react to it by just doing more of what I want to do. I take *more*."

The room was quiet again as they both considered this.

18:44 | CAKE

"I still can't quite get over being able to walk out of the house without setting up an entire support system," said Liz. "Lists of food, emergency numbers and so on."

"Yes."

"I've recently taken on a fantastic amount of work, and I'm really looking forward to it."

"Yes."

"I tell you it's not vanity that's the issue, is it—it's employability. Keeping your place in the world. I want to carry on working. I'm doing the best work I've done in my life but—and I notice it every time I go for an interview— fifty is a black mark. They think you're their mum!"

"I'm going to get one of those fish throats, I can see it coming," said Mae, pinching her neck pensively. "My mother had one so I don't see how I can avoid it."

"What do *you* say now, Mae, when people ask your age?"

"Sometimes I tell them to mind their own business," said Mae. "Sometimes I just stare at them. But I really don't care. I don't have to; it doesn't affect my work. What do *you* say?"

"I say, guess! As in, guess the weight of the cake in the village tombola. In fact, I do think if they ask your age they should insist on your weight as well—it's just as relevant to your health and fitness for the job."

"I don't think that would catch on," said Mae. "I don't think that would be very popular."

"Imagine if they stood there trying to guess your weight aloud as if you were a cake at a village fete!"

"Yes . . ."

18:48 | BLOOD

Mae stood holding Liz's forearm in a pulse-taking clasp, motionless as a statue.

"All this talk," said Liz. "And we're not even there yet. At least, I don't think I am. Are you?"

"No. Not really. Though I find there's a new unpredictability."

"Yes."

"Funny, though," said Mae. "When blood appears after a long pause—seven weeks recently—I feel pride.

Blood makes me feel strong and powerful. I'd hate to have another baby now, but it makes me proud to know I still could."

"Yes."

Yes, it would be strange to leave this behind, thought Liz; even at the times when internally she had been melting and trembling, crumbling, with hot joints, hot swollen breasts, it had been being in another state. But these new tides of thin heat flowing just under her skin, like shadows racing over hills when clouds cross the sun—these were interesting too. Inconvenient sometimes, but interesting.

"And now that the drama of our fertile years is drawing to a close . . ." continued Mae.

"Melodrama, more like."

"Will you mourn it? Will you mourn it as a little death?"

"*Petite mort,*" said Liz. "That's what they call orgasm in America, isn't it."

"Not in France?"

"I think they say *jouir* in France, as in, to enjoy. It's weird to call it a little death, I think, when the actual experience is more like waking up."

"I thought it meant epilepsy," said Mae. "*Petite mort.*"

"That's *le petit mal.*"

She had even come to look forward to it over the years, each time it came round, the volatile week. Yes, it could be a nuisance in practical terms but sometimes she felt cleverer, she felt as though she saw and understood more . . . Nor was it false, the thin-skinned emotion that emerged at such times. Extravagant more like, so that life appeared as lurid and backlit as an El Greco. Not untrue; not to be acted on, either.

"As for mourning it," she said now, considering Mae's query. "I suppose it's time passing, another step towards the grave if you see things in those terms; but I don't. No. Not unless it means I'll somehow feel less intensely; not if it means emotion will become less powerful."

"I don't really see why that should happen," said Mae.

"What I wouldn't want is to get very cut-and-dried; you know, very blunt and dismissive and set in what I felt about everything."

"No."

"But then again, sometimes I think I really wouldn't mind feeling less," said Liz perversely, with feeling.

They fell quiet, separately musing.

"I envisage the new state as being like Arizona," said Mae at last, opening a new packet of needles.

"Arizona?" said Liz, nonplussed.

"Yes." Mae shrugged.

"What, a desert?"

"No, not that. I see it as . . . It might be . . ."

"Phoenix. Tucson. Why *Arizona*?"

"I see it as arriving in another state," said Mae, slowly. "Brilliantly lit and level and filled with dependable sunshine."

"Oh!"

"In fact, I can't quite believe in it," said Mae. "This promise of . . ." She stopped again and fell silent.

"So that's it," said Liz. "We're about to emigrate."

It's true, isn't it, she thought. Already I'm not as quickly moved to tears as I was ten years ago; soon I'll have cried all my tears and only laughter will be left.

18:55 | RISORGIMENTO

Mae walked round the table, peering closely at Liz's face and hair as she extracted the long needles one by one.

"Do they ever break off?" asked Liz, raising one hand gingerly to feel.

"Never," said Mae firmly.

"So I won't find the point of one in my scalp tonight when I come to wash my hair?"

"No! It doesn't happen. The needles are very fine but they're very strong as well. Now, careful as you sit up. Slowly."

"Yes," said Liz as she swung her legs off the edge of the table. "Oh! I feel really clear-headed. Alive."

"Good. Now, would you like to see how it goes or book a follow-up appointment?"

I want to go ahead unashamed, thought Liz as she reached for her bag. Is that possible? Unashamed. Brave! At the very least brave, because you've got to be. At every stage really, looking back, and this is no different. Except now there's no need to fit in because for the first time there's no particular template.

"I don't want just to accept it—I mean to enjoy it," she declared to Mae. "I like being here, now, this minute."

"Well, we're all living in time," said Mae, glancing at her watch. "That's fifty pounds, please."

"Cash, isn't it," said Liz. "I went to the machine on the way."

"Thanks. Women our age—it's different now, it's not the image that's put out, is it. Look at us! We're strong and active, we've raised children and earned money all our lives; we're fine. Look at you with your big lecture next week on . . . what was it?"

"The Risorgimento," said Liz.

"Yes. And while you're getting dressed, it's supposed to be a good thing as you get older if you can put on your socks or tights without sitting down or leaning against anything."

"What, like this?" laughed Liz, standing on one leg like a flamingo, unsteady, one arm flailing for purchase in the air, teetering, hopping from side to side, finding her balance.

"Yes," said Mae, laughing too. "Like that."

BERLIN

DIENSTAG / TUESDAY

"Remind me why we're here again," says Adam as he watches their companions decant themselves slowly and more or less painfully from the minibus.

"You know why," says Tracey.

"We must be twenty years younger than any of this lot. Thirty in Trevor's case. And Olive's."

"Fifteen," says Tracey, smiling at the others as they approach. "Thirteen? Less. Pauline can't be more than, er, sixty-eight. Anyway, don't be such an age snob."

"Trust my parents!"

"It's been a hard year. You needed a break and this was booked and paid for."

She notices she still has his best interests at heart so she probably won't be able to leave him. But they really can't go on like this. Can they?

Their seats reserved for this *Ring* package are at the back of a raked box of six ranked in pairs. In the middle row are Pauline and the venerable Olive—two sensible white-haired widows, Tracey supposes them to be—and in front of them the bearded ones, Howard and Clive.

"I hate opera," says Adam.

"You said you'd keep an open mind," says Tracey.

They had originally agreed to accompany Adam's mother here over a year ago. The *Ring* cycle, his late father's favourite, would be the best way to mark what would have been their diamond wedding anniversary, his mother had decided: suitably epic and time-consuming. Not long after booking it though she had herself died, and they had had to watch another coffin glide towards the flames. Meanwhile Culture Vultures, true to their name, would refund only one ticket of the three.

Much of the time Adam's father had shut himself in his den and kept the household cowed by blasting out Wagner at full volume. He had resented the very existence of his children, according to Adam and his brothers; he would simply rather they had not been born and had made this quite clear during the years they had lived under his roof. Then, when at last in middle age his sons had felt brave enough to ask him why, he had beaten a hasty retreat down the corridor of dementia; as Adam had said to Tracey at his funeral, four years ago, "It's like he had some South American bunker waiting in the jungle."

"I hate opera," he now says. "And I *really* hate Wagner."

"Look, we'd both booked the time off work," says Tracey. "And we haven't exactly got money to throw around."

"I know, I know," he says.

She hopes this won't set him off on his current favourite hobby horse, how as an architect he has made so much less money than his brothers in insurance and advertising even though he'd been cleverer than them at school. Luckily he has been deflected from this path.

"Just look around at this lot," says Adam. "They're all so delighted with themselves for being here. They make me sick."

"Let's make the best of it," says Tracey. "Think of it as a challenge, like Everest."

"What, a feat of endurance?"

"Why not. You like a challenge. And a change is as good as a rest."

"Huh!"

"Also, Wagner is supposed to have unearthed the deep stories of Germany and I for one want to find out what all the fuss is about. We're European, aren't we?"

"Are we?"

"Well, I am."

"OK, OK," says Adam, flapping the programme in front of his face. "We're here now. Stuffy, isn't it."

Tracey looks out across the auditorium and registers the predominance of snow-topped heads. Even you've gone grey, she thinks, glancing at Adam's angry profile.

"No interval," he says, finding the English language section in the programme for *Das Rheingold*. "They're having a laugh! Two and a half hours straight through?"

"Um, the Culture Vulture notes say this is the short

one," says Tracey, finding them in her handbag and scrabbling for her reading glasses. "This is like a prelude to the other three. Do you want to know what they say about it?" She does not wait for an answer. "In a nutshell . . . Greed for gold, greed for property and power means breaking contracts, losing love, going against nature. Quasi-Marxist analysis of society; elements of a creation myth; da da da, remarkably prescient on climate change."

"Oh, great. Climate change as well. Wonderful. That's the icing on the cake!"

"Look, the lights are going down. It's about to start."

"Can't wait."

"Let's get lost in the story," she whispers, taking his hand. "The surtitles will carry us through."

Silence. Then, from nothing, from almost nothing, from one long low chord, there grows a gradual swell of sound, a rising tide of it, and the stage is slowly flooded with rippling blue-green light. This is beautiful. It's like the beginning of everything all over again. Tracey relinquishes his hand and touches the side of his face. His mouth twitches in a reluctant smile.

Ah. Oh dear. Three stout singers in shiny bodysuits have arrived and they're singing very high and loud against the noisy orchestra. That's wiped the smile off his face. What do the surtitles say? "Wagalaweia! Wallala, weala weia!" What sort of language is that? And now, "Lass' seh'n, wie du wachst!"

Oh my God, the surtitles are in German: she realises this at about the same time as Adam, who turns towards her with an expression of silent outrage.

Well, there is nothing she can do about it now, is there.

Gradually she jettisons the ballast of the day and her thoughts start swimming out into the flood of this nonstop music. After a while she realises this is not like other operas she knows. It's not like The Marriage of Figaro or Rigoletto; here the orchestra is on the go the whole time. There aren't the usual distinct arias and duets.

"It's all so unnatural, opera," Adam had complained earlier.

"Once you get that what they're singing is their inner thoughts rather than normal speech then it's a breeze," she had told him.

The big luxury is making yourself understood and in ordinary life that's asking too much. It can't be done. Nor are they going to understand much of what's going on here without surtitles.

It is having a strange effect on her thoughts, sitting here drenched in sound, so that they unfurl in unaccustomed slow motion, not fleeting at all. Random memories present themselves for inspection as though they have been waiting for this space in which to unpack themselves. On the radio last week she had heard a scientist talk of new brain imaging systems that would mean all your emotions and reactions to life could be logged and placed alongside others at your death: a library of souls. *Ha,* she thinks, *there's bound to be an app for that* soon. They say, Why let the past drive the future? The past is over. Yes. But I think it's like a piece of music, particularly this sort of wraparound music. You're in it, inhabiting it. What you remember, though, and what you want, they change too, don't they? She glances at Adam's set and angry profile. This ill-suppressed bad temper, she thinks, the inadequately fire-blanketed rage; they're no fun to live with.

Onstage now there is a new scene, a middle-aged couple lying side by side asleep. For some reason they bring to Tracey's mind the couple who had been in front of them at the airport check-in desk that morning, a retired builder and his wife. A good two decades further down the line than her and Adam, they were off to Miami (they had confided) for a Caribbean cruise; last year they'd had to go from New York because of the weather and had spent two nights on a concrete floor, snowed in until after a mad late dash they'd caught the cruise with only five minutes to spare: what a nightmare!

So why would you volunteer for the same again, Tracey had wondered; two nights on a concrete floor in your seventies doesn't sound much fun. Then, as the woman had continued with details of the final close-call cab ride to the ship, her face animated, proud even, she, Tracey, had understood that it was their first adventure of the year as each year rolled round and that its value lay in sharing the adventure with each other.

Adam might mock but the fact that everybody else on this trip is of pensionable age will serve to make them both feel younger by comparison, surely? He's right though, at least two of the group are well into their eighties: Olive, in front of them *now, and Trevor, with his somewhat younger wife, Denise, somewhere in the stalls. Yes, a* Ring *package is obviously ideal if you've had a hip replacement.*

The couple onstage have risen from their bed and they're quarrelling already. Now he's leaning on his spear and glowering while she goes on at him. The habit of resentment, the habitual tone of injury (thinks Tracey), they've caught that well. All long-lasting loves have their betrayals. Obviously. We're human beings. And who's to say blocking or blanking them is any worse than blame-laying and excoriation?

Their parents' generation had been dead set against what they called "wallowing." They had practised denial on a massive scale, refusing to talk of painful memories, believing that if you blanked the past for long enough it would disappear. Denial! It was supposed to be a harmful thing and yet it seemed to have worked well enough for that generation, which was after all the most long-lived so far in the history of the world.

The men on stilts have grabbed the golden girl, she's struggling but it's no use. Off they go, dragging her along with them. The stage darkens. The ones left behind have started to stagger and hobble around, they're not looking good. Who knows what's going on? Tracey hasn't got a clue. Adam looks at his watch.

Everyone is getting so old but at the same time they're careering around all over the place instead of hunching down by the fireside; and the thing about travel is that it does make your time seem longer. She thinks: I'm always amazed at how long and alive the days are when I'm away, even when they're unenjoyable or tiring. Today has lasted almost a week so far by that count.

Onstage the scene is dark and confusing: is it a salt mine, perhaps, or a mountain cave? Various men cavort and bellow, backed up by the tense excited swarming of violins, the blare of horns.

This is like swimming (she thinks), or like when you're surfing pleasurably on the sea of sleep, lucidly dreaming, at that point of not being quite ready to wake up. Or a bit like being at the cinema, the waking dream element. A novel demands five hours plus from your life and that's quite cheeky—more than a film or a play—but you can take it at your own pace. Whereas Wagner makes you all sit in the dark together then turns the key on you.

He must have been madly egocentric, an insane bully, to insist on such vast tracts of time from his audience. What an enormous act of ego, to expect people to put aside the best part of a week of their lives for this cumulative event! He's managed it though, hasn't he. He's dead but here we all are sitting in the dark locked at his behest into this whatever-it-is.

It is over at last. The curtain calls have been lengthy and the applause ecstatic but in the end the lights have come on. Tracey stretches and rubs her face, refreshed after her long swim in this unaccustomed sea. Adam has hated it though.

"Bellowing, bullying," he says. "Balls-achingly boring. Just like Dad."

In the minibus on the way back to the hotel there is a flurry of talk. Tracey closes her eyes and listens to it with Adam glowering at her side like a thundercloud.

"What on earth was going on in the scene with the helmet?"

"It turned the dwarf into a toad, not that you got to see that bit."

"Oh. Right. No, not entirely clear."

"I think Loki's supposed to be Bismarck, rather confusingly."

"But what was it *about*? What was the plot?"

"It's about what happens if you don't pay your builders on time."

"What builders?"

"The ones on stilts."

"The ones that kidnapped the girl?"

"Freia. Yes. Eternal youth."

"Eternal youth! I could do with some of that."

"Couldn't we all."

This makes Tracey smile and she opens her eyes.

"Hard to know what's going on without surtitles," says Trevor, the most genial of the voices. "If you don't know the story."

"Yes, I do wish Culture Vultures had given us the translation in with their notes," says Tracey.

"Good notes otherwise," says Clive. "Decent little potted history of Germany and a vocabulary list of sorts."

"Rather eccentric," says Howard. "Those notes smell of some half-mad underpaid postgrad to me."

"Smart-arse," mutters Adam in Tracey's ear.

"Earwig!" says Trevor. "What was this earwig they kept singing about?"

"Yes, *ewig*," says Tracey, "I noticed that too. I'm going to Google it when my phone's charged."

"*Ewig* is 'eternal,'" says Olive unexpectedly.

"You speak German?" asks Trevor. "Good woman! You'll be useful to have around."

"Not *much* German, I'm afraid," says Olive. "I've forgotten most of it by now. I lived in Lübeck for a while, back in the mists of time."

"I was jotting down words in the dark," says Tracey. "On my programme. Words that kept cropping up. Here they are. *Zorne, Zwänge, Zeit.* They seemed to come in clusters, several words all beginning with the same letter. *Zauber!*"

"*Zauber* is 'magic,'" says Pauline. "I know that from *The Magic Flute.*"

"*Vertrag, Verrat, Versprechen,*" continues Tracey.

"Yes," says Howard. "It's full of alliteration, his libretto."

"Alliteration," says Trevor. "Hale and hearty. Forgive and forget!"

"*Vergeben und vergessen,*" says Olive.

Back at the hotel Tracey lets Adam go on ahead while she waits at reception for the return of their passports. Trevor is there too.

"Personally," he says, once they have them, limping along the corridor towards the lift with her, "I think Wagner single-handedly ruined good opera. Verdi's the man! Wagner's a curse—ghastly fellow, morbid, hysterical, wallowing in death and disaster."

"Oh dear," says Tracey. "So you can't be looking forward to—?"

"Denise loves Wagner," says Trevor. "And I love Denise, so let's keep that little secret to ourselves. But certainly it proves how much I love her, doesn't it, that I'm ready to spend a week of my life, at my advanced age, on Hitler's favourite composer, horned helmets and all."

"Impressive!" says Tracey.

He is a skilled old flirt too, she notices.

"Look at us!" she says, standing beside Adam in front of the bathroom mirror. "We're like one of those paintings: the Triumph of Hope over Experience. Or should that be the other way round?"

"Oh, very funny," he says. "Ha ha."

She grimaces at their reflection in the mirror.

"Over fifty and you're into the Land of the Uglies. It's like arriving at a fancy-dress ball, isn't it, where they make you put on a pair of comedy glasses and a fright wig."

"Did you get the passports?" he says.

"Yes. Trevor was there as well. I like him. He's not too keen on Wagner either."

"It's a gigantic case of the emperor's new clothes, that's why."

"Adam, why not give it a go?"

"Why should I?"

"Because! Why not!"

"That's not a reason."

"Oh my love, you are your own worst enemy."

He is almost asleep. It's no good, she must speak.

"I want to forget, but it's still there," she murmurs into his shoulder.

He groans. "Not this again."

"Please help me."

"Water under the bridge."

"I know but it won't go."

"Look, Tracey, I have certain areas where I just tend to think 'trouble' and put them in a locked drawer and leave them alone."

"I know."

"I don't like turning things over."

"Neither do I but my mind keeps on doing it anyway."

"Let's get some sleep."

"I've never talked to anyone except to you; and you can block your ears to me."

"It's after midnight, Tracey. Oh don't cry, for God's sake."

"I'm not."

They are quiet for a while.

"Our love," she murmurs. "That's what I couldn't

understand you sacrificing and seeming not to notice. It seemed so strong to me."

"It still is!" he says. "Go to sleep."

In the night Tracey wakes and stares into the dark. The tormentors are ready for her. I've been living as though my life wasn't important, she thinks with nighttime clarity. Now that the boys are older, now that they are in the outside world, it changes all the conditions. She resigns herself to the fact that she will not be able to fall back asleep, not for a while at least. Malaria is like this, isn't it; you think it's gone then it comes back again. Once it's in the bloodstream you can't get rid of it.

Enough, she says to herself, climbing noiselessly out of bed and reaching for the notes and her bag. She goes to the bathroom, softly closes the door and turns on the shaving light instead of the main one so that the extractor fan won't wake him. Good, it's strong enough to read by. She closes the lid to make a nocturnal chair, and turns to her Kindle; within seconds she has it downloading a translation of the *Ring* cycle's libretto. Next she starts browsing the notes.

INFORMATION: There are eighty-three opera houses in Germany; the cities and regions have much more power than in the UK over their own budgets and they do the bulk of the funding. There is very high musical quality even in smallish houses and because there are so many of them many more people can go and enjoy the opera. Also the ticket prices are nowhere near as high as ours.

QUOTATION: "Wagner's art is the most sensational self-portrayal and self-critique of the German character that could possibly be imagined; as such it is calculated to make German culture interesting even to the most doltish foreigner." From "The Sorrows and Grandeur of Richard Wagner" by Thomas Mann, 1933.

ODD FACTS: Wagner wore glasses all the time, only removing them when he had his photograph taken. Kaiser Wilhelm II, who abdicated three days before the end of the First World War, had his car horn tuned to the thunder motif from Wagner's *Ring* cycle.

VOCABULARY: *Hoch in der Luft*–high in the air; *hoch in den Siebzigern*–in one's late seventies. *Bildung*–the lifelong process of education and self-cultivation; *Stolperstein*–stumbling block. *Leitmotiv*–in the musical drama of Wagner and his imitators, a theme associated throughout the work with a particular person, situation, or sentiment; a recurring theme. *Traulich und treu*–tender and true; *der feindliche Freund*–frenemy; *in wildem Leiden*–in bitter sorrow; *heilige Ehre*–sacred honour.

She takes her holiday notebook and copies out this new vocabulary, then turns to her phone and starts to Google the recurring words she had jotted down from that night's surtitles onto her programme. Yes, *ewig* is eternal, as Olive said, and *Ehre* is honour and *Eid* is oath or marriage contract. *Vertrag* is contract or agreement, *Versprechen* is promise and *Verrat* is betrayal. *Verraten und verkauft,* the translation service further volunteers, is "well and truly sunk." She sits there for the best part of the next hour, resigned to wakefulness, reading and copying German vocabulary into her notebook.

MITTWOCH / WEDNESDAY

They are among the first of the group to assemble in the hotel lobby, Olive and Pauline and Tracey, in readiness for the coach tour.

Breakfast had been full of trombone-like nose-blowing from the older men along with the odd percussive sneeze. When Adam had helped himself to a bowlful of what looked like good honest muesli from the buffet table, the depth of his chagrin on finding the dark bits were chocolate rather than raisins had been worryingly disproportionate. Was this her future, Tracey had wondered aloud back in their room: hair-trigger breakfasts with an angry old man? If so she would be bailing out sooner rather than later. Having thus provoked a brief but savage exchange from which she had come off worse, it is with some relief that she has dried her eyes and left him fuming in their room checking his emails.

"Hello, my dear," says Olive. "We were just talking about the voluminous notes with which we have been provided, and how we haven't yet found time to read them."

"I know, I only started reading them last night," says Tracey. "I never knew there were eighty-three opera houses in Germany!"

"That many?" says Pauline. "They can't be much good if there are so many of them."

"I'm not sure that's the case," says Olive. "I have a dear friend in Magdeburg and whenever I've visited her I've been to the most wonderful things. A stunning *Idomeneo* last time."

"Oh well, it's all new to me," says Pauline. "Since I retired. I always used to think opera was just for snobs but when they started those screenings live from the Met, then other opera houses and theatres too, I got hooked. That's where I saw the *Ring* the first time round, at my local cinema in Wrexham."

The lift disgorges Clive and Howard. Clive acknowledges them with a smile while Howard takes out his phone and starts to check it.

"Adam's father was mad on Wagner," says Tracey. "He had to leave school at fourteen during the war but one of his old teachers kept in touch and used to lend him books and records. That was how he picked up the Wagner bug; he was obsessed."

"A not uncommon story at the time," says Olive, nodding.

"Something of a golden age for autodidacts after the war too," says Clive, who has been listening. "Myself included. No music in the house when I was growing up, not even a radio, then I discovered the Proms! I went every week in summer for next to nothing; the Albert Hall was my second home."

"Yes, the Proms. And the Old Vic," sighs Olive. "Gielgud for a shilling! What a wonderful woman Lilian Baylis was."

"Up in the gods at Covent Garden for half a crown," says Clive, glancing over at Howard. "Meat and drink to us at twenty."

Ah, that's where they met, Tracey realises, all that time ago: up in the gods.

When everyone has arrived they go outside to where the coach is waiting.

"Sorry," whispers Adam in Tracey's ear as they wait for the others to get on first.

"Thank you," she whispers back, sliding two fingers between his shirt buttons to the warmth of his stomach beneath.

"I'm hungry," says Adam. "That chocomuesli at breakfast was a disgrace."

"It's important to make the most of these lunches as

we won't be getting any dinner," says Howard, forking in a mouthful of buttery *Kartoffelbrei*.

"Yes, they must do double duty," says Clive at his side, busily sawing away at his pork chop. "Good job they're included!"

The group is at lunch after a long morning's coach tour of Berlin.

Why on earth had anyone thought it a good idea to do that to Berlin after the war, Tracey wants to ask. Berlin was Prussia's capital, wasn't it, and Prussia had been behind both world wars. What was Bonn, then? But really, why had Berlin needed to be circumscribed, quartered and reduced to a nervous breakdown after the war, and kept that way in a permanent state of psychosis for all those years? It's way over in the East so why had the West kept a toehold here at all? Embarrassed at her own confusion, she knows she is not atypical of her generation in her reluctance to give a backwards glance to the waste and wastedness, the wastefulness of war. Their parents, still below fighting age in 1945, had been the opposite of nostalgic and their grandparents had never wanted to talk about it. Yes, you had to pull your legs out of the mud somehow and climb free if you wanted any future to happen to you.

"I read that book on Berlin in 1945 before we came out here," Trevor says. "What's the writer's name? It'll come to me. Good book but depressing. Terrible what happened to the women."

"Trevor," says his wife, Denise. "We're eating."

"And certain things are only coming out now, all this time on," he continues, shaking his head.

"Torsten liked the sound of his own voice, didn't he," says Pauline.

"I'd had enough of him by the end of it," says Adam.

"I must say I felt the same," says Olive. "Rather a hammy performance."

"Berlin has also a bad side and I want to tell you this," intones Clive with a theatrical lift of the eyebrow. "And as you know we are now governed by a *woman*. The Queen of Europe. You can *have* her. Or should we send her to New Zealand?"

Everybody is laughing; Clive has caught Torsten's tone and words with some accuracy.

"Repetitive too," says Adam. "Should we remember, should we forget, he played that number at least half a dozen times."

"They've been going in for atonement in a big way recently," says Howard.

"The sins of the fathers," says Clive.

"They're in overdrive if anything," continues Howard. "They've grown so keen on fessing up that they've started in now on their colonial sins in a way that puts the rest of us to shame. They're streets ahead of us there!"

"Yes, it was interesting what Torsten had to say about the new Humboldt museum," says Olive.

"Whereas I thought Checkpoint Charlie was very disappointing," says Pauline. "Russian dolls, Russian hats, hot dogs in the drizzle."

"Good to see that bit of the Wall though, wasn't it," says Trevor. "Extraordinary! All those years then the Cold War melted away overnight."

"There's a bit of a chill in the air again now," says Clive.

"More like a hard frost!" says Adam.

Tracey notices that he seems happier, and helps herself to a second glass of wine.

"It's so weird that Germany wasn't even one country until about a hundred years ago!" she says to Clive on her left. "Like Italy. I was reading the notes last night. All very confusing. The Thirty Years War, the Seven Years War, the Schleswig-Holstein question."

"Ah yes, the Schleswig-Holstein question," says Clive.

"Our pick 'n' mix system of teaching history doesn't really work, does it," says Tracey. "Everyone does the Tudors and the Nazis but not much else and there's no before and after."

"Very true," says Clive. "Chronology's gone out of the window."

She sips her wine and senses ideas and feelings jostling for room inside her head. She is remembering a recent television programme on what had happened in Germany after the war; the misery, the shame, the cruelty . . . The orphaned infant children of Nazis and others living wild in the forests, like a horrible Grimms' fairy tale; the dogged attempts to sort through the rubble and build replicas of what had been before, as if that could restore the past in some way.

"We're so lucky, aren't we. But it makes me feel . . ."

"I know," he says. "I feel incredibly lucky to have reached my age and not to have had to live through a war."

"All that misery, though," says Tracey, putting her wineglass to her hot face to cool it. "Catastrophic. It makes me feel ashamed of having feelings at all . . . How dare we feel happy or sad! What do our puny little sorrows matter set against that? Do you know what I mean?"

"Yes," says Clive, pouring her a glass of water. "But they do."

"You think so?"

"Of course. Your own life continues to be important to you. It's all you've got!"

"I suppose so."

"Definitely."

"This one's got two intervals," says Tracey. "Good."

"It's also a lot longer," says Adam.

They are back in their box, in the back row again, waiting for *Die Walküre* to start.

"The notes do say it's always been the most popular one with audiences," she says. "So that's promising."

"Right," he says, slumped in his seat already.

"A band of warrior women, you'll like that. And there's a wild man of the woods, he's Siegmund."

"Siegfried?"

"No, Siegmund. As opposed to Siegfried, who's in part three. Yes, confusing. Anyway, he falls in love, Siegmund does, with his long-lost twin sister, Sieglinde."

"That's enough, thanks."

"Give it a chance."

"I don't know why you're making excuses for it. It's inexcusable."

At the first interval he races ahead to queue for drinks. As she dawdles on the stairs she is still caught in the music of that last scene, a door flung open and moonlight flooding in on its tide. *Mond,* she thinks to herself: moon. In her mind's eye she sees the delicate and powerful moonlit scenes from early that afternoon, a roomful of paintings by Caspar David Friedrich in the Alte Nationalgalerie. In the rooms after that there had been a higher than usual incidence of antic skeletons, deathbed scenes and funerals. "They're a bit samey after a while, aren't they," Adam had said. "Let's skip them." Surprised by the luxurious emptiness of the gallery, they had also found its attendants strenuously zealous compared to their counterparts in London. As soon as she had stepped into the first room a man in uniform had stopped her and mimed reproval with his wagging finger—her handbag on its shoulder strap must not be worn hanging to one side but must be slung across the front of her body. He had also demanded to see their tickets, the first of five attendants to do so in these almost-empty rooms during their visit of less than an hour.

Finding a space now at one of the high circular tables near the bar Tracey leans against the edge and turns on her Kindle. She is half-listening to the conversation opposite. Business types, they look, so it will be client entertainment; an English couple with their German host.

"You have been to Covent Garden?" asks the woman, rather loudly and slowly, as though to a deaf person.

"Yes, yes," the German replies. "It is very fine!"

"And did you see many differences between there and here?"

"Not many. But one thing I was shocked—the people putting their coats under the seats."

"That is true," says the other man. "It's compulsory to check in at the cloakroom here, isn't it. But we like to make a quick getaway, you see!"

"It's sort of Heavy Metal meets the Pre-Raphaelites, isn't it," she says as Adam appears beside her.

"More like *Snow White* meets the *Odyssey*," says Adam. "It's a mess."

"I was meaning the audience more than the opera," says Tracey in a lower voice. She points out a number of Wild Men around them. While the women have short hair or sensible bobs, even the young ones, it is the men who monopolise the attention with their ponytails and beards.

"And do you see how little colour they use? They're all in blacks and browns and greys, the women as well as the men."

"Less frivolous than us," says Adam, scanning the room briefly.

"But there is one bright colour they go for. The women, the ones who wear colour at all. Look—do you see?—it's that harsh scarlet that looks no good on any-body: sex-shop red."

"Yes, you're right," he says, following her gaze.

"Red Riding Hood chic," she says, referring to a shop window they had paused at that afternoon on their walk back to the hotel from Museum Island.

"Extraordinary," he says, shaking his head. "Talk about bedtime stories."

The window of the sex shop had displayed a manne-quin clad in short scarlet hooded cloak and thigh-high patent leather boots, a wicker basket over her arm and a six-foot-high cardboard cut-out of a leering wolf behind her. In the top corner of the window was a black-and-white photograph of a smiling woman in flying helmet and goggles. Oh, I've read about her, Adam had said. She's a national institution, she really was in the Luft-waffe during the war, a proper Valkyrie; then she set up this string of sex shops and made a fortune.

Nothing much seems to be happening, she thinks now as she gazes at the stage. Half an hour into the second act and Adam is already asleep. There is a lot of self-justification and brow-beating in this bit, the Kindle has revealed, and not a lot of action.

Yes, Fricka is fidelity and she's a bore, an uptight bore, but she's got right on her side. Unfortunately. Whether or not you live by the same code of honour as each other (thinks Tracey), whether you are mutually exacting, keeping each other up to scratch or—more commonly—one-sidedly so, like Fricka and Wotan; this is the question.

Fricka's noble wounded look is cutting no ice, is it. Being hurt and good is not enough. Righteous indignation is a mug's game. Oh (she thinks), but I want to feel simple generous warmth again and the desire to give!

This music is like dreaming; it's like a waking dream, the way her thoughts are wheeling round the sky, hoch in der Luft, and the way time is swelling and expanding. Where are her old greedy self-pleasing daydreams? Dreams come first, before anything can happen you have to dream things into being. Desire is the motor so listen to it, she tells herself sternly; it can be damped down so hard over the years that it gets hopelessly lost.

Now Fricka is giving Wotan a hard time. Nag, nag, nag. What a thankless role. The whole institution of marriage is a bit Prussian, isn't it; an oath of fealty; the public regulation of the private life. Under contract! Signed and sealed and silenced. Yes, loyalty inevitably seems to involve silence (she thinks) and perhaps that's what music is for—it's emotion in the air.

Beside her Adam gives a little snore.

Wotan is a bore too, though. He wants to have his cake

and eat it. Now he's boring on to Brünnhilde, a long screed of self-absorbed self-justification. On and on, he's worse than Fricka. And Brünnhilde's got to take it. She's his daughter; she's supposed to respect the arbitrary authority of this mixed-up old bully.

Adam's father had been jealous of his boys and rivalrous, enraged by any little successes they had had and furtively savage in the ways he cut them down to size.

Where was Adam's mother when all this was going on? "She should have protected us from him," he had once said. "Not him from us." Yes, that's an undersung part of the duty of parents, thinks Tracey now: each must, as necessary, protect their children from the other.

All gone now, though, their parents, and really it did not seem that there was very often an easy way out of this world.

"That was a bit sudden," says Adam as they make their way to the bar area. "Wotan just waved his arm at the end there and that other one fell down dead. The one in the leather greatcoat."

"Oh, you were awake for that bit, were you?" says Tracey. "It was pretty boring, though, that whole act, to be honest. Except at the end, then suddenly it was mayhem in the last three minutes."

"Yes, it got quite noisy then, didn't it. That's what must have woken me up."

"He's gone off the rails, Wotan, he's in deep trouble. Here's our table and here are our drinks. Good idea, ordering them ahead. Shall we do a bit of speed-reading now on the Kindle to help with the last bit?"

"OK, as long as you keep clicking on."

"'*Hojotoho! Hojotoho!*'" Tracey reads aloud. "'A flash of lightning breaks through the clouds, revealing a Valkyrie on horseback. From her saddle hangs a dead warrior.' That's right, that's what they do, isn't it, swoop down on battlefields and scoop up dead heroes to bring back to Valhalla."

She looks up and catches the eye of the young woman opposite her at the table.

"We need a translation," she explains, holding up the Kindle. "We cannot understand the words."

"No more can us!" replies the woman to laughter from her companions. "The words of Richard Wagner, we cannot know what they mean!"

They look merry and nervous and friendly, this little group in their thirties, on a night out enjoying themselves.

"Let's get this straight," says Tracey. "Brünnhilde is Wotan's daughter, right?"

"Yes!" the group replies.

"And Siegfried is his grandson?"

"Yes, yes!"

"It's incest?"

"It is incest."

"So they're doomed," says Tracey to general mirth.

"It is, what do you say, interbreeding," one young man explains earnestly.

"The Habsburg jaw," says Adam, thrusting out his chin and baring his lower teeth at him.

The young man recoils in alarm.

"Everybody knows this bit, it's famous," whispers Adam into Tracey's ear as they lower themselves into the third act. "It's in Apocalypse Now, *it's the bit where they go in with the helicopters." On the warpath, thinks Tracey; death as sexy. No, it's not, it's really not. It's never sexy. The dead are nowhere. They're nothing.*

And yet. And yet here they all are, held in the music of a dead man. Making something out of nothing, she thinks, something that didn't exist before; that's what this is. Babies are how most people do it, but they don't last. Death is the opposite: it makes nothing out of something and it lasts for ever.

How brave it had been of her father when, given a week or two to live, he had spent them ringing round to close his various accounts. "Very messy, probate," he had explained. He was a practical man and had wanted to make things easier for her mother once he'd disappeared. "You'll have to wait seven to ten working days," the Nationwide girl had told him, reacting at first with incredulity and then with shock at the other end of the phone when he had explained why that might not be possible.

These warrior maidens are impressive creatures, Brünnhilde and Waltraute and the rest, noisy and vigorous (thinks Tracey, watching them as they leap around and wave their weap-

ons). But in the end they're good conformist girls. They're doing what their dad tells them to do. They're warlike, yes, but they're never going to end up in charge and they don't want to be in charge or even imagine being in charge. Loyalty, deference, obedience—these are their values. When it comes to it, though, is loyalty even a virtue? Or is it just a brainless self-abrogation, a slavish abandonment of responsibility? It's a matter of belonging, perhaps. But where's the intrinsic virtue in being loyal to your team or your father? It all depends on what you're being loyal to; it's no use at all if you're being loyal to the wrong cause.

The way this music tells you how to feel, brooking no opposition (she thinks), it's like the way film music goes to work. Here they are again, those gorgeous phrases from before, rising, swelling, imposing their own rhythms; and here's that other theme, overwhelmingly beautiful, drawing up from the depths your own long-lost childhood feelings of entrancement and grandeur. The sound is vibrating through your body, invading your nervous system (she smiles uneasily at this thought). It is like being in love: fascinating. Something powerful is in the air, you can't see it or touch it but it has taken control at the wheel.

It's over. She starts to come down with some reluctance from the ravishing music of the last twenty minutes or so, and nudges Adam to open his eyes. Wotan has punished his favourite daughter for disobedience by striking her unconscious and surrounding her with fire. All round Brünnhilde little jets of flame sprang up like the rings on a gas hob, she tells him on the way down the stairs; but, oh dear, some of them *had gone out again before they were supposed to and the stage finished in a shroud of dry ice.*

"The Valkyrie costumes were a disgrace," says Pauline once they are all packed into the minibus for the trip back to the hotel. "Those poor girls! Nazi uniforms, biking leathers: ridiculous."

"Such a lazy cliché," says Olive. "I quite agree."

"And the pole dancing didn't work either, did it," says Clive. "They definitely looked out of their comfort zone there."

"Was it supposed to be like Torsten's facing up to the past?" says Tracey. "Though if so it wasn't followed through. I mean, if the Valkyrie were the SS then Wotan should have been Hitler."

"Fricka as Goering," scoffs Howard. "Erda as Goebbels."

"Torsten really didn't approve, did he, of having women in charge," says Tracey.

"Yes, he was very scathing about the minister of defence being a woman," says Pauline. "I read somewhere she's a doctor and she has seven children."

"Seven!" says Tracey. "That's ridiculous."

"Personally I find it rather reassuring," says Olive. "There are no mothers to speak of in the *Ring*, of course. Certainly not any good ones. Though in the end redemption is achieved by the Eternal Feminine."

"The what?" says Adam.

"Ah," says Olive gravely, turning her head to look at him. "It's Goethe."

"Clive and Howard were both teachers," says Tracey, combing her hair at the bathroom mirror. "At the same school. And Olive used to teach piano before arthritis got into her hands."

"What about Pauline?" says Adam beside her.

"She started in retail, she told me, then she set up some sort of mail-order business later on. She's interesting."

"You think everybody's interesting."

"No I don't. It was a good day though, wasn't it?"

"It was OK. Yeah. The East and the West, and seeing what's left of the Wall."

"Twenty-five years ago," she says, "I was holding Matthew, he was two months old. I was feeding him and watching it on television, the Wall coming down. Now he's twenty-five and it seems like the blink of an eye. I can remember my life before them, the boys—pretty much the same amount of time. I've still been childless for longer than I've had children. Just. Same goes for you."

"Mmm," says Adam, who is now cleaning his teeth.

"Everybody was so happy, do you remember? Without breaking eggs! The first time in history!"

"Mmm."

"Do you remember where you were? I know you were out."

"Training session," he says, spitting into the basin. "Another lifetime. Hung my boots up now."

"But if that's the blink of an eye, twenty-five years, it's only four blinks to be back at the start of the First World War. When our grandparents were children."

"Come to bed," says Adam from the bathroom door.

"Remember how when the boys were little the best bit was always having a solid weight to sit on your lap and put your arms round? Do you remember?"

"You put yourself and what you wanted first, always," says Tracey, lying in bed in Adam's arms.

"That didn't mean I didn't love you."

"I suppose that's true."

"I still do."

"Yes."

"You'd have done a lot better if you'd been more like me."

"We wouldn't still be married if I'd been more like you."

"You must have really wanted to stay married, then!"

"I thought I could change it."

Adam heaves a gusty sigh.

In the night she wakes and stares into the dark. As aches and pains stay with old soldiers, reviving fifty years on with changes in the weather, so these thoughts rear up to meet her in the small hours. I was frightened of doing harm, she thinks; I didn't realise I'd end up harming myself instead. Wide awake now she decides to take her notebook and phone off to the bathroom for another small-hours session with the notes and Google.

INFORMATION: The world's first voluntary monuments to national shame include the Memorial to the Murdered Jews of Europe (2005) on a five-acre plot in plain sight of the Reichstag (meeting place of the Bundestag/German parliament). Across the road in the Tiergarten are three more such memorials, much more modest in scale, to groups hunted down by the Nazis: to homosexuals (2008), the Roma (2012), and the disabled (2014).

QUOTATIONS: Einstein in Berlin in 1919 compared Germany to "someone with a badly upset stomach who hasn't vomited enough yet." The last line of Kurt Weill's *Berlin Requiem* is, "You do not matter and you can die without worrying about a thing."

ODD FACT: With the noble solemnity of the Valhalla motif in mind, Wagner commissioned a new instrument to be made: the Wagner tuba is somewhere between a trombone and a French horn.

VOCABULARY: *Blick*—glance; *Trauer*—grief; *verdorren*—wither; *Waldmann*—man of the woods (hunter, forester). *Blut und Eisen*—blood and iron; *Blut und Boden*—blood and soil; *Totentanz*—dance of death. *Vergangenheitsbewältigung*—the struggle to come to terms with the past; that's much too long, thinks Tracey, how are you meant to get to grips with that one. Whereas *Das Kopfkino*—the skull cinema, the thought-pictures which unroll in your head when you're daydreaming—that one will come in useful, that's what's going on during this week's lengthy stretches of music.

DONNERSTAG / THURSDAY

"Forty-eight hours of food like this," says Trevor, eyeing the substantial piece of beef on his plate with pleasure, "and it's straight on to the antacids."

The group is seated at a large table in the Reichstag's restaurant with a panoramic view towards the east.

"It's good though," he adds. "Yes, they like their meat in Germany, don't they."

"Not all of them," says Adam. "Wagner and Hitler, they were both vegetarian."

Denise, whose vegetarian option sits wilting in front of her, looks glum.

"They're all fascinated by their digestion," says Howard. "Like the French. But whereas the French worry about their livers, with the Germans it's their bowels."

"Regularity!" says Olive. "That was the word they used to use when I was a child. You had to be *regular* in England before the war. They were obsessed. Oh, the dreaded syrup of figs!"

"They call it detoxing now," says Tracey. "Cleansing the intestine."

"The body doesn't really work like that, of course," says Trevor, taking a slurp of his wine.

"Constipation," says Olive. "Another word you don't hear anymore."

"Though when something does go wrong with the digestion," says Trevor, "it can be quite hard to spot exactly what's the problem. Speaking as an ex-medic."

"I'm always convinced indigestion is a heart attack," says Howard through a mouthful of beef.

"You bolt your food," murmurs Clive, shaking his head.

"When mine went wrong last year," says Trevor, "I was pretty sure I knew what it was. From the symptoms, though, there was something else it might have been too and they wanted me to have tests to eliminate that possibility first. Which I did. And, as I thought, it wasn't that."

He pauses to help himself to mustard before continuing his story.

"Then they said, 'We'll open you up and have a look.' Which they did. And indeed it was what I'd said it would be—a gangrenous intestine."

"That sounds bad," says Tracey politely.

"In the event it was fine, they caught it in time and

removed a great stretch of my gut. But you're right, it could have been very nasty."

There is a pause while they all digest this. Adam puts down his knife and fork and looks out of the window towards the TV Tower.

"Impressive, I thought," says Pauline, changing the subject. "The way they've preserved that Russian graffiti–and left it on display there for all to see. It's not exactly complimentary."

"*Hitler kaputt* was the only one that nice girl could bring herself to translate for us," says Olive. "She hadn't bargained with the notes!"

And indeed the notes had provided full translations of the various obscenities in Cyrillic script.

"I must say I was very struck by the glass dome," says Clive. "I hadn't realised that anyone at all can walk up there and watch the MPs debating in the chamber below."

"Good old Norman," says Adam. "It takes a Brit."

"Yesterday on the bus tour," says Tracey, "did you notice as we drove past the British embassy that it was surrounded by massive stone blocks? Just like the American embassy in Grosvenor Square. We're obviously the ones seen as warmongers now."

"Yes," says Olive.

As their plates are cleared to make room for Black Forest gateau, the talk turns to tonight's opera.

"It was Wagner's own favourite from the *Ring*," says Howard, getting into his schoolmasterly stride. "It's the most obviously fascist of the four. The blond hero who is simply a superior being. Though the fact that fascism didn't exist when Wagner composed it counts for something. And it does all go wrong."

"This big blond hero business," says Pauline briskly, "it's more Scandinavian than Germanic, surely. Wagner was small and dark, wasn't he?"

"Like Hitler," says Adam.

"The Nazi ethnologists did in fact have Wagner down as Nordic-Dinaric," says Howard. "The Dinaric bit from the Balkans. And certainly he comes across as more Celtic than Teutonic. As for Hitler, he adored the *Ring;* he carried the manuscript of the music around with him everywhere."

"Was Wagner your special subject on *Mastermind*?" asks Adam.

Howard ignores him.

"Did you see that film about Hitler?" asks Trevor. "Very good, I thought."

"Rather a lot of films about Hitler," says Adam.

"You're right," sighs Trevor. "Let me think. I mean the one where he's in his bunker. The name will come to me. Eventually."

"The one with Goebbels and his wife and they kill all the children?" says Pauline. "*Downfall,* do you mean?"

"That's the one!" says Trevor, beaming with pleasure.

"Der Untergang," says Olive.

"Cyanide pills," says Clive. "Now there's an opening for an entrepreneur. Someone would stand to make a fortune if they could find a way to sell them online. There's a big market there for something quick and easy, rather than having to go to Zurich."

"Not sure how *easy* cyanide is," says Trevor. "No. North Sea gas, now, that used to be relatively straightforward; head down and off you went. But that option disappeared long ago."

"It's clearly a good idea to have something up your sleeve," says Olive.

"Downfall," Howard says. "The film, I remember thinking, they'll use *Götterdämmerung* for the music. Bound to. But no! Not a bit of it! They took that great English hymn to suicide instead, *Dido's Lament!*"

"Remember me!" Clive sings out in a reedy voice. "Remember me!"

"So what have you got up your sleeve, then, Olive?" asks Trevor.

"Well, I have heard the water from a vase of foxgloves is very effective"—Olive smiles—"so I make sure to keep my garden well stocked."

"Aha!" says Trevor. "Digitalis!"

"What?" says Adam.

"Shhh," says Tracey.

They are deep into the third opera and Tracey marvels at the casual violence of this lighthearted lunkhead Siegfried. He is recognisably Viking in his boisterous brutality, isn't he, and as Howard has now told them more than once, Wagner's main source material was from the Old Icelandic. So much for the deep stories of Germany. Adam is awake, though, and seems not to be hating this one.

The Eternal Masculine, she thinks, remembering Olive's phrase from the night before. Siegfried is bold and fearless. That's what makes him the hero, the strong man. And even now the strong-man myth holds sway.

This Wagnerian urge to idolise and hero-worship is actively harmful, she thinks; I know that, I've always known it. Wotan may be king of the gods but he's a bad-tempered depressive as well. Siegfried is strong and handsome but he's a blithering idiot too. Shun shamans! Once I'd grown up (she thinks) and learned to live with the idea that strong emotions can also be ambivalent, I was laughing. And crying. Not everyone has a simple nature.

So (she wonders), are clear-sightedness and the state of being in love mutually exclusive? Because when you fall in love, that transformative state which is like music, then there has to have been idealisation. A degree of distance. Not falsification, but not the whole truth either. Not at the start; no.

Here comes the blame-laying Wanderer in his floppy hat, spreading doom and gloom. Her memory reels back to the conversation she and Pauline had had that day in the Reichstag; sotto voce, she recalls, as such conversations between women on this subject usually are, rather than out in the open, to avoid being shot down in flames.

"Blame-laying," she had said to Pauline. "Establishing who's in the wrong."

Adam had missed their guidebook and, fulminating against

Tracey, had left them together while he ran off to look for it at the table where they had all just eaten.

"Something comes unstuck that's not my fault and I know I'll have to fight like a demon if I'm not to get the blame every time."

"My sons do it too," said Pauline. "It's not just him. It drives me insane."

"How do you mean?"

"I shout at them, 'And? So?'"

"How?"

"Meaning, fine: you've established where the blame lies, but so what? The real question is, what are we going to do about it? But they're less interested in that, they're far more interested in blame-laying. Whose fault it is. All that."

"Yes!"

It emerged that they both had two sons. Pauline spent much time visiting hers, and their children, and getting blamed for things; children are always angry at their parents for something or other, she had said with a shrug.

"Are yours competitive?" Tracey had asked. "With each other? Mine are."

"Mine don't even speak to each other, they're so competitive! They're grown men, married, with mortgages, but that doesn't make a blind bit of difference. One runs a marathon one year, then the other one finds out and signs up for two marathons the following year. And now they've both signed up for this ludicrous Ironman challenge."

"Ironman?"

"You wait, that'll be next. It's a two-mile swim followed by

*a hundred-mile bike ride followed by a twenty-six-mile run, in
that order, without a break."*

"Oh my god."

*"It's the latest thing to add to your CV apparently. Gives
you that extra edge."*

*Siegfried would have breezed through the Ironman chal-
lenge, him and his sword, which he has, of course, forged
himself. And now he's killed the dragon with it.*

"That took a while," says Adam, appearing at her side
during the second interval with the drinks. "Lots of Brits
in the queue. The woman next to me told me she was
in a coach party from Colchester, forty of them, they'd
bought their tickets online in a block booking and they're
going on for a meal afterwards. She said this is their sev-
enth *Ring* cycle!"

"They must set out to bag them like Munros," says
Tracey.

"Addictive, even I can see that now," says Adam. "This
music, listening to it here with you, it's quite different
from being blasted with it by Dad. It's very rousing. Quite
a lot of the time in the wrong way, though, it feels like."

"How do you mean?"

"In the Nuremberg rallies way, I suppose."

"Oh. Yes."

"I like sitting beside you. Being with you."

"Yes?" she says.

"Yes. But let's get back to the Kindle, Tracey. OK. Siegfried argues with the Wanderer, that's his grandfather in disguise, isn't it. And he chops his spear with his sword."

"There's the bell; skip to the end," says Tracey, leaping ahead. "Siegfried kisses Brünnhilde awake. Song to the sun, the radiant day. Love at first sight, la la la. But then she worries. For two, three, four pages about losing her independence, her armour."

"You were like that. Remember?"

"With reason," says Tracey. It felt like you were going to be giving up a lot more than the man, she remembers, getting married. The world, in some sense, as well as your freedom. You had to be able to trust him as a friend. Or was that just my generation of women?

"There's the bell, we've got to go," says Adam, gulping down his wine.

"Last lines," says Tracey, her eyes on the Kindle as they hurry back up the stairs. *"Leuchtende Liebe, / lachender Tod."*

"Meaning?"

"Radiant love, laughing death. That's what they both swear to each other."

"Laughing death?" says Adam. "Are you sure?"

"Shhh," says Tracey. "It's starting."

Tracey dreams and drowses inside the music, rocked along in its turbulent reverie. Time to move on (she thinks); fine, but if you have done harm it is indelibly part of your history from then on. If you're interested in being truthful. It just is. Sometimes sitting on a bus could be like this, couldn't it; the noisy chugging and purring, stopping and starting, like moving along inside a giant teakettle, slow progress, the lack of end in sight, your fellow passengers sitting alone in their private fastnesses, bags on laps, but also companionable by virtue of simply being there.

If you listened to this on your own, as Adam's father had done, you would be taken through a huge emotional experience with none of the usual human real-life fallout. You'd be able to avoid thinking about damage, you'd be able to concentrate on the quality of your own emotional experience without being selfish or mean to anyone else. It really could be all about you!

"He stuck it out for whatever reason," she had said to Adam that day about his father. "He didn't leave."

"So what. He got no joy from us. It all had to be about him or it didn't count."

"I know. That's sad."

First her parents, then Adam's. It was like that party game where the ones who are touched on the shoulder must sit down silent, inactive, out of it. She thinks of children alone in their beds, breathing like the sea.

Ewig again, they are singing, and again: Trevor's earwig; eternal, everlasting. She thinks: we seem to stay the same, or reasonably like ourselves, for years and years and years. But time is marching on, or up and down, or round and round; whatever. How to meet death, that was what you had to think about once you were no longer a child—first the deaths of others, then your own. Yes, bear it in mind; but the real skill was not to let it dominate your thoughts. These strange meanderings (she observes), this lofty abstract afflatus, they're a direct result of contact with this music, aren't they; its elephantiasis is obviously catching.

Trevor had been telling her that day how much he enjoyed his life. "I've got enough money," he'd said, "I've got my health, I've still got my marbles, and it's wonderful now to have enough time to do the things I enjoy." Trevor and Olive are to be admired, the spirited old travellers. Over eighty and you're in another country, living in the court of a despot, hoping to escape notice for as long as possible though you know that sooner rather than later you're for the chop.

The way this music catches at you again and again with certain chords and phrases repeated ringingly is part of its power, signature phrases which cycle round again and again like the emotions. Tears had sprung to Olive's eyes that day when questioned about her time as an infant evacuee during the war. And is it ever possible (Tracey wonders) to detach emotions and send the painful ones back into the slipstream of wither and fade? They don't seem subject to the usual rules; they don't acknowledge time.

This music is loudly physical (she thinks), repetitive, and it vibrates through your whole body, the blare of the horns, the roll of the drums. It creeps in and enlarges itself, feeding on itself. It alters your heartbeat!

She takes Adam's hand and they are palm to palm, fingers laced and straight and moving slightly to the music. Now she slips one shoe off and slides the sole of her unshod foot along his shin, moves the arch of her foot up from his ankle and *round to his calf. In their box, safe in the back row, he takes her warm hand, both of them shifting silently, smiling politely, conscious of each other and of those in front of them. She thinks of the night to come. All she has to do is touch his skin, touch it softly and with imagination; all she has to do is touch him with her fingertips softly and sensitively . . .*

It is quiet tonight on the minibus back to the hotel; they are tired, the members of this little group, and some of them have their eyes shut.

"I know we were complaining about the lack of surtitles," says Pauline to no one in particular, "but I'm rather glad of it now. I already know enough of the story from seeing it in the cinema so I'm not bothered about it. This time round I find I'm listening to the music undistracted. And it's amazing."

Tracey takes out her notebook. *Ausgang*/exit; *Stuhlgang*/bowel movement; *Untergang*/downfall: these she has added to her vocabulary list today. From the Kindle she now copies out the lines which had appealed to her at the beginning of the last act: *Mein Schlaf ist Träumen, / mein Träumen Sinnen, / Mein Sinnen Walten des Wissens.* My sleep is dreaming, / my dreams are thoughts, / my thoughts master wisdom.

"We used to have vocabulary books at school," says Clive. "Ten words a day. French rather than German, though. *Jusqu'au bout. Une crise de nerfs.* Very useful."

"It's supposed to be good for the memory, isn't it,"

says Trevor beside her, "learning a new language. Though I do the crossword instead."

"I can't do crosswords," says Tracey. "I wish I could."

"I must let it go. I know that," says Tracey.

"Yes!"

"I will but I need something first. From you."

"Revenge? Is that it?"

"No. I don't want that."

"What then? Reparation?"

"No. Not that either. Recognition? Yes! Recognition. Say you understand what you've done and chose to do it even though you love me and knew it would hurt me."

"Ah, that's a bit hard. I just did what I wanted and I didn't think about uncomfortable things."

"Please. No need for remorse. But there must be recognition."

"You want to be the one who's in the right. OK. I'll give you that. You can have that."

"No! I don't care about that either. No, it's so I know what happened, so I know something more about you and we can carry on from there."

"I don't want you to know that about me."

"Well, tough."

"Let's change the subject," says Adam, and kisses her with such energy and persistence that she cannot say anything else.

In long married life, reflects Tracey later, before she

falls asleep, foreplay is not so much a formality as a formalised, stylised process, elegant in its gestures. It is in that way like a traditional dance worn to a fine edge, new heights, by centuries of repetition. And there is always the possibility of surprise, of some movement or sensation quite new, not experienced before.

SAMSTAG / SATURDAY

"Of course, we're all living longer," says Adam. "That's the problem."

"Quite a nice problem though," says Trevor. "When you get to a certain age."

Tracey smiles across at him, and he winks back. The group is having lunch in a Turkish kebab house before the final stretch of this operatic marathon.

"I had my seventy-fourth birthday last week," announces Howard. "And I did one of those online quizzes that tell you how long you've got. They get better, the odds, the older you get. It's because of the people who've dropped off already on the way. So actually at seventy-four you've got more chance of living to a hundred than you had at sixty!"

"I don't see how that works," says Adam.

"The first time I did it I was somewhat economical with the truth when it came to entering alcohol amounts," continues Howard, ignoring him and taking a swig of wine. "And I came out at ninety-seven. Then I went back and filled it in more truthfully and I still came out at ninety-five!"

"Adam's right though," says Trevor. "The health service is in a terrible pickle. Because not only are we living longer, hurrah, but the treatments available are so much more effective and of course so much more expensive than they were twenty, thirty years ago . . ."

"And as for pensions . . ." says Adam.

"Adam," says Tracey.

"When I retired at sixty I was advised to plan for ten thousand days," says Pauline. "Part of the retirement pep talk they gave us."

"That's interesting," says Howard keenly, starting to do the sums.

"It's going to be more like seventy for us," says Adam. "If then. Pensions have turned into a disaster area."

"I was reading something yesterday," says Tracey hastily, "when you were all in Potsdam and Wannsee, and it said the First World War lasted fifteen hundred days."

"Eighty-seven," says Howard to Clive, pursing his mouth.

"This is one of the best kofta I've ever eaten," says Trevor. "Now, *Götterdämmerung*! What does it actually mean?"

"The twilight of the gods," says Olive.

"Oh, of course," says Tracey, reaching for her notebook. "*Dämmerung* is twilight!"

"A somewhat ominous reputation, this one," says Clive.

"Yes," says Howard. "It trails a strong whiff of Eau de Bunker."

"Though surely a lot of that's down to bad luck," says Pauline. "Like 'Nessun Dorma' and the World Cup."

"Just one Cornetto," warbles Clive.

"But then all sorts of goodies were claimed in the name of the Third Reich," says Howard, steamrollering over them. "The glory that was Greece, the Brandenburg Gate modelled on the entrance to the Acropolis, they took all that on wholesale. The Olympian master race."

"Oak trees," says Clive, "forests. The Wandervogel youth movement."

"The what?" says Adam.

"Rambling," says Clive. "The Nazis were very ecologically minded."

"I thought the oak tree was old England," says Adam.

"No, no, the Germans got there long before us," says Howard.

"Are you sure?" says Adam, frowning.

"Absolutely sure."

"But that doesn't make oak trees bad," says Tracey. "Just because Hitler liked them. Or the Acropolis."

"Or, by that logic, Wagner," says Howard.

As the coffee stage arrives, Tracey asks to swap with Clive so that she can sit between Olive and Pauline.

"Hello, my dear," says Olive. "So where did you get to yesterday while we were visiting Potsdam?"

"And Wannsee," says Pauline, shaking her head. "Grim."

"I'm afraid I'd had enough of Torsten so I skived off," says Tracey. "Though I'm very glad I did, as it happens."

She tells them how she had wandered off Ku'damm down the Fasanenstrasse and stumbled by chance into the Käthe Kollwitz Museum.

"Käthe Kollwitz?" says Pauline. "That name's familiar though I don't know why. I think I noticed her name in the notes, that must be how I know it."

She extracts the notes from her bag and starts searching through.

"A great artist," says Olive.

"I know!" says Tracey. "I know now, anyway. I'd barely heard of her before, I only knew her from a couple of lithographs and I thought I was keen on art."

She thinks back on what she saw and wonders how she is going to express any of it to them. Nothing had prepared her for this house; she had wandered in a trance through rooms of tender terrifying lithographs and woodcuts showing Death bringing comfort to starvelings, Death seizing a group of children, portraits of hungry children and desperate widows, women holding sleeping children, dead children, and scenes of lamentation. She had found herself knocked breathless by the angry power and honesty of these pictures, by their furious mother-love and strength.

"Things she said," she continues. "I copied them into my notebook from the captions. Here. 'I have never done any work cold. I have always worked with my blood.' When she was fifty and famous she took on the Kaiser and publicly denounced the war—here we are, 'We were betrayed then, at the beginning . . . Peter and millions, many millions of other boys. All betrayed.' *Verraten*. How brave to write that in the papers in 1917! Why is she not more famous outside Germany?"

"'Seedcorn must not be ground,'" says Olive, somewhat obscurely. "And of course she went through the Second World War too. A thorn in Hitler's flesh. She died two weeks before it ended."

"Käthe Kollwitz," reads Pauline from the notes. "Here we are: 'Berlin's guardhouse memorial to the victims of war and tyranny,' da da da, both the Communists and the West tried and failed to claim her as their own. Lost a son in first war, a grandson in second war, both named Peter. 'Her massive bronze pietà of mother and dead adult son lies above the remains of an unknown German soldier and an unknown resistance fighter in soil from nine European battlefields and five concentration camps.'"

"From her last diary," says Tracey. "'One day, a new ideal will arise, and there will be an end to all wars. I die convinced of this.'"

"I wish I could," says Olive.

"Yes, a double espresso please," says Pauline to the waiter now taking their orders.

"*Schwarzen Kaffee, bitte,*" says Olive.

"We'll be needing caffeine if we're going to last," says Pauline. "We get on the minibus at three fifteen and we're picked up again at ten."

"But, Olive, what I really meant to ask you about was that thing you mentioned," says Tracey. "The Eternal Feminine. Before I got sidetracked."

"Das ewig Weibliche," says Olive. "Yes."

"What is it? What does it mean?"

"Redemption," says Pauline witheringly. "Compassion. I'm willing to put money on it! It makes me so mad, the way we're always fobbed off like that."

"Yes," says Olive.

They are in the back row of their box, for the last time, shoulder to shoulder.

"Have I got the gist?" asks Adam, while Tracey clicks through the Kindle's pages. "Siegfried does the dirty on Brünnhilde but it's not his fault because his drink was spiked?"

"I think that's it. *Blutsbrüderschaft.* Blood brotherhood. Yes. Here we are. *Gram und Grimm. Hoy ho, hoy ho, hoho!*"

"And this new villain Hagen," complains Adam. "It's a bit late in the day to be introducing extra characters!"

"Though it's still mainly Siegfried and Brünnhilde. Here she is: *Verrat! Verrat! Wie noch nie er gerächt!* Treachery, treachery, needing unprecedented revenge!"

"And the magic helmet making him look like the other one—how on earth are we going to follow all that?"

"Close your eyes during those bits, that's what I do. Listening to the music like that, it's like dreaming."

Dreams, she thinks as the lights go down—unrealistic rub-bish (in terms of story) except for the emotion. And here comes this music again, the music of transition; shifting, always changing. She moves her shoulders and relaxes back into her seat. Over five hours, this last one; nearly six if you counted the intervals. It does have a cumulative effect, though. How familiar it is to her now, after swimming in it all week; familiar and new.

Repetition with variation, she thinks; the same but dif-ferent. That elderly couple at the airport had understood it, forging a new inner world together via shared adventure. You didn't need to go that far, though; anywhere new would do as long as it was new to you both. And how is it that even though we sit at the end of the Atlantic storm track, one day of sun leaves us convinced that summer's here? That's why we still make resolutions and think of new ways to approach life after all this time: because we're human and we need to be reminded and encouraged and refreshed. Again and again. Right to the end.

Do you want to get old? (she asks herself). Well, yes. I've grown increasingly attached to my life and friends and loves as time has gone on. I want to see what happens next. When young, you're not tied in in the same way; you're not yet rooted. Remember the baby's first three months of fragile hold before they're quite in the world? Even up to thirty or so the death of a parent can blight the not-quite-rooted young. I remember saying to my mother, laughing, "It's all right, you can go now. I hope you don't. But I'm fine on my own, I'm grown up now."

Wehe! Wehe! Waffen durchs Land! Horns are sounding and there is a lot of running around onstage along with the waving of spears and swords. She glances at Adam and sees how absorbed he is; over the course of these four long nights in her company the colour and information and weave of the music have persuaded him. Olive had that day described to her how she had struggled with the language during her brief married spell in Germany, making fruitless painful efforts to pierce the wall of impenetrable sound in which she had recognised only the occasional word; and then how, not gradually but all at once, she had realised she could understand what people were saying. It had been like tuning in to an elusive radio station, she said. And that's how it's been this week with the music, Tracey thinks; even Adam has got his ear in, which is quite something considering his Wotan complex.

Olive had assumed a hooded look when questioned by Tracey and Pauline about her time in Germany. "Never live with a depressive, they suck your life away," she had said, adding that in her view marriage was what you could put up with but now she had many dear friends. It was all that time ago in Lübeck too that she had discovered opera—"I found it was where I could do my violent living, my antisocial living," she'd told them. "It's saved me a great deal of real-life mayhem like that."

"And that's obviously the way your dad used it," Tracey had said to Adam, repeating this last remark to him. "He might have been a lot worse without it."

Look at Brünnhilde! She's just given her husband's secret away to the villain! Now he's had it. Tracey thinks: but wasn't

*she supposed to be the redemptive power in all this? How is
that redemptive? Burning with hurt and rage she betrays him.
It's murderous, her betrayal.* Verrat! Verrat!

*She lapses back into drowsing again, abandoning the
attempt to follow the confusion onstage. Lying beached on
Adam's shoulder last night, aware of the barrel of his ribs
rising and falling with his breath, half asleep, she had seen
in this liminal state which hovered at the border of sense
how there are between life partners sliding layers of history,
tectonic plates of it shifting over the decades together.* Verrat, *how could there not be* verrat *in all that time, with two
separate temperaments side by side and often wanting different things; experiencing disparate degrees of satisfaction
with whatever they are together living through to the point of
sometimes withdrawing, almost bailing out, for long stretches
of distance. The hurt, the very imprint of betrayal, its cause
all but forgotten now, phoenix-like revives and burns, flares
up again. What happens is neither progress nor its opposite
but a cycling round again through the emotions; not cloudless,
never cloudless except for simpletons or deniers. And, in the
middle of all this, claiming some sort of essential freedom
while remaining loyal—how hard was that?*

"Gallingly slow these days, I'm afraid," smiles Trevor, seeing Tracey on the stairs at the second interval.

She returns his smile and slows to his snail pace.
Where is Denise?

"I find I need to touch a wall or rail now or I keep veering off," he continues. "There goes Olive, beetling along, beating me to it every time and I happen to know she's a couple of years older than me."

"How are you finding this one?" asks Tracey.

"Well of course it's rather magnificent. But between you and me I'm still finding it a bit . . . screechy."

"Is Denise enjoying it though?"

"She seems to be as far as I can tell. You may have noticed she's been rather silent this trip, and again between you and me, she's got to start chemo straight away when we get back."

"Oh dear. I didn't know."

"No, she doesn't want to talk about it. She skipped through a knee replacement recently with flying colours. But she's also had lupus for several years now, rather debilitating, and she's ten years younger than me so of course it all seems a bit unfair."

"Yes. Though fair doesn't come into it, really, does it. That's up to the Norns."

"The Norns?"

"Those three at the start tonight."

"The ones with the knitting?"

"Yes, the three Fates."

"That's what they were! I wondered what all that was supposed to be about."

"The past, the present and the future."

"Ah yes. I see. So fingers crossed for us they don't drop a stitch, eh?"

"Yes!"

When you're in good health it's like living in a time of peace (thinks Tracey as the lights dim for the last time); you don't notice it, you don't think about it, you take it for granted. And happiness is when you're not aware of your health; it's when you can think outside yourself. No wonder Denise has been so silent.

She senses how a chronic illness can take the shine off each new day in advance, how it may—if not treated in time with distraction tactics—lead to cool thoughts of ending it. Which is of course one way to ameliorate the idea of self-obliteration, though not one you'd necessarily choose. No.

The three big Rhinemaidens are back onstage with their lovely music, something of a relief after Hagen's dark bass hoi-ho-ing. This is the last act of all and everything must be decided.

At this late stage in her life she could no longer sit indoors and watch television, Pauline had told Tracey after lunch that day, which was pretty much all she'd been fit for round the edges during forty-odd years of work and family life; no, she wanted now to explore what she hadn't had time or freedom for in the past. She had also confided in Tracey that there was someone on her art course she could not stop thinking about and how she was thinking of leaving her husband for this person. "As long as I'm alive I'm a work in progress," Pauline had declared. "The way I see it, I'm alive until I'm dead."

On stage they are building a bonfire and it is quite obvious where things are leading. Brünnhilde is looking exalted as she sings of her impending immolation. It's grandiloquent and babyish at the same time (thinks Tracey), this desire to see it *all go up in flames! The urge to take everyone down with you, not being willing that anything survive unscathed after your own death—this is the titanic selfishness which Wagner is obviously recommending. But this hysterical insistence on perfection in death where no change is possible: it's all a big fat lie. You have to live with the past whatever action you decide on, and also history can change. If you can't for now agree on a version of what happened, though, you can't go forward either together or separately. And it's sinister, it's anti-human, the demand for absolute control over the story.*

Here's Brünnhilde doing the decent thing though; all done and dusted, nothing left to chance. The confusion onstage doesn't make this entirely clear. Adam is looking baffled. "Suttee," she whispers in his ear, and he turns and raises his eyebrows at her in surprise. So incontrovertibly thrilling is the music, however, that by the end they find themselves convinced.

They are all quite elated tonight on the minibus back to the hotel; there is a feeling that they have seen through some great enterprise together. Also, time has become finite again as they are going home tomorrow. Tracey closes her eyes and lets the talk go on without her, leaning on Adam, who has his arm over her shoulders.

"Why were they waving that big sheet across the stage at the end?"

"I think it was supposed to be the Rhine breaking its banks."

"That must have been the climate change bit. Flood and fire."

"Not sure what the moral is though, now that it's come to an end."

"Mind your back?"

"I liked the bit where his dead hand lifted."

"I missed that! Siegfried, you mean?"

"On his pyre, yes. Or was it his bier."

Opening her eyes, Tracey reaches for her Kindle.

"His last words!" she says. "Do you know what his last words were? Seriously creepy. Look, here they are: *Süsses Vergehen, seliges Grauen*—To die is sweet; to shudder is enchanting."

"Yes," says Pauline, grimacing.

"And I don't see how Brünnhilde can be the heroine," says Tracey, "if she ordered a hitman. Olive, she had Siegfried murdered!"

"At the end," says Olive, "she's supposed to get on her horse and ride bareback into the flames. Not long after I was born there was a production in New York where Brünnhilde was played by a great singer who was also a great horsewoman, the Australian Marjorie Lawrence. She rode a real horse right onto the stage and into the fire. It was the sensation of the season."

"What happened *after* that, right at the end?" says Adam. "By the way. Something was definitely going on but it was out of our sightline."

"Valhalla went up in flames."

"Here it is," says Tracey, reading from her Kindle.

"Bright flames set light to the hall of the gods. When the gods are completely hidden from view by the flames the curtain falls."

"We were on the wrong side," says Adam, aggrieved. "It was out of sight where we were sitting. Just a faint glow!"

"Ridiculous," says Pauline. "Half the opera house couldn't see it."

"We got a good view from our side," says Trevor. "Whoosh!"

"Like the ending of *Jane Eyre*," says Tracey, "Thornhill on fire. And Manderley of course! *Rebecca*."

"Last night I dreamt I went to Manderley again," says Denise unexpectedly.

The women laugh gently together.

" 'I won't think of it now. I'll think of it tomorrow,' " says Pauline in a southern drawl. " 'After all, tomorrow is another day.' "

The men look baffled.

" 'Reader, I married him,' " says Denise, taking Trevor's hand.

He beams at her.

"I didn't exactly *like* it," says Tracey. "That seems the wrong word altogether. But I did think it was tremendous."

"Yes, that's how I feel about it," says Adam. "You see, we do agree, always, about the important things."

"Well, whatever happens in the future this will be part of our history," says Tracey.

"I'm glad I stuck it out," says Adam. "But I'd never want to sit through it again."

"Rather how I feel about marriage."

"Oh, ha ha!"

Having packed and washed, they fall into bed like two felled trees—an oak, it might be, and a lime tree—their branches pleached.

In the night one partly wakes and then the other. She is more than half asleep, velveting her face inside his shoulder. They are about to drift off again when he murmurs his thoughts aloud.

"If I had my time again I'd do things differently."

There is silence.

"No, I don't think you would," she breathes at last.

"I would!"

"But we don't have our time again. Ever."

"No more talk of leaving," he says. "Think of the boys! You couldn't do that to them; it would be like dropping a bombshell on them."

"Shush."

"No sending it all up in flames, Tracey."

"Go to sleep."

"We're about to get old. Any minute now."

"I know."

"When one of us dies the other one won't have this anymore."

"I thought that too."

They grow quiet again for a while, except for the sound of their breathing, rhythmic like the sea.

"As long as I've got you," he says.

There is no answer.

"Tracey?"

This time though it seems that she is the one who is first to have fallen asleep.

Acknowledgements

"Cockfosters" and "Torremolinos" were originally published in the *Guardian*. "Erewhon" was originally published as "Night Thoughts" in *Granta*. "Kentish Town" was originally published as "The Chimes" in *The Times*. "Kythera" was originally published as "Cake" in the *Telegraph*. "Moscow" was originally published as "Strong Man" in the *New Statesman*. "Cheapside" was originally published as "Ambition" in the *Financial Times*. "Arizona" was originally published in the first issue of *Freeman's,* October 2015.

A NOTE ON THE TYPE

This book was set in Garamond, a typeface originally designed by the famous Parisian type cutter Claude Garamond (1480–1561). This version of Garamond was drawn by Günter Gerhard Lange (1921–2008) and released by the Berthold type foundry in 1972. Lange based his Garamond revival on a combination of models found in specimen sheets from both Paris and Antwerp.

Claude Garamond is one of the most famous type designers in printing history. His distinguished romans and italics first appeared in *Opera Ciceronis* in 1543–44. While delightfully unconventional in design, the Garamond types are clear and open, yet maintain an elegance and precision of line that mark them as French.

Typeset by Scribe, Philadelphia, Pennsylvania

Printed and bound by Berryville Graphics,
Berryville, Virginia

Designed by Betty Lew